BED AND BREAKFAST AND MURDER

Book One: The Fiona Fleming Cozy Mysteries

PATTI LARSEN

Cover design by Christina G. Gaudet

www.castlekeepcreations.com

Edited by Jessica Bufkin.

ISBN: 198870006X
ISBN-13: 978-1988700069

ACKNOWLEDGMENTS

With my deepest thanks to:

Jessica Bufkin
Christina G. Gaudet
Elisabeth Kaufman
Scott Larsen
Kirstin Lund
Lisa Gilson Noe
Caron Prins

From the bottom of my heart, for saying yes.

CHAPTER ONE

DOING BATTLE WITH A clogged toilet was not how I expected my Thursday morning to start. In fact, I had a whole lot of not much in my sights, a veritable plethora of nada, zippo, blessed and delicious time to myself. Hot coffee fresh from the pot, the latest edition of the *Reading Reader Gazette* spread out on my kitchen island, pajamas still gracing my weary self as I slowly and with great relish devoured a mushroom omelette without a hint of interruption.

I really, really should have known better. It had only been two weeks, but honestly. Owning a B&B was like wrangling a house full of two-year-olds who alternated between cranky demands and petulant whining topped with the biggest messes I'd ever seen in my entire life.

Case in freaking point. I tried not to look down the mouth of hell staring back at me from inside the glaringly pristine outer ceramic shell of the white throne, my throat catching, stomach doing half flips and a rather impressive rollover routine that would have gotten at least a 9.5 even from the Russian judges. Instead, I forced myself to smile and swallow and remind myself the elbow length yellow rubber gloves grasping the handle of the standard issue plunger were all that stood between me and Pooageddon.

A few jabs and weak efforted prods did little to clear the clog. Time to get a bit more vigorous, put my back into it. The soft groaning yawn behind me made me spin with a scowl on my audience of one.

"Do you mind?" I flipped back my auburn bangs, blowing at them to keep them out of my eyes while the portly fawn and black creature staring up at me with bulging eyes huffed in response. "I'm working here."

Petunia snorted violently, spraying little flecks of moisture on the white tile floor before perking her black ears at me, her squish pug face an equal mix of utter innocence and complete disdain for my present predicament. It wasn't that it was her fault by any stretch, but she was here and enough of a reminder I'd said yes to this place *on purpose* I almost tossed the plunger at her.

Suck it up, Fee. Big girl panties and adulting and all that. I glared at the pug and then myself in the mirror as I turned back, catching the wrinkles forming between my eyes despite my twenty-eight (okay, soon to be twenty-nine, but who's keeping score) years, the tightness of the skin around my bright green gaze. At least I'd had the foresight to put my heavy hair in a pony. The very thought even a scrap of myself could touch that mess unprotected made me want to shave my head.

"At what point," I waved the dripping plunger at myself, wincing as droplets of yuck flew, "did I think owning a bed and breakfast was going to be glamorous and romantic?"

Petunia yawned, whining in her pug way for me to get on with it then. Jaw clenched and determination in my heart, I went to war.

I found a rhythmic rocking motion seemed to gain me ground, grunting added for good measure. And swearing, lots of swearing. Blaming, too. The damned tourist who decided to use half a roll of toilet paper to clean his precious butt. Mary Jones, my always glass so empty she was dehydrated elderly cleaning lady for telling me in no uncertain terms this was my job. To quote: "I don't plunge toilets." And my Grandmother Iris for having the temerity to think that I, Fiona Fleming, city girl who hired a cleaner twice a month so she wouldn't have to touch dirt would be good at the domestic disgustingness of taking over her prized B&B after she died.

Yes, swearing helped a lot. And actually created energy, oddly enough, as did the horribly phallic feeling action of my labors. As long as no one was videotaping this, I'd pretend it never happened.

Ten minutes later, panting and sweating and, I'm sure, wearing some of the contents of the toilet and unwilling to admit it, I stood triumphant over the offensive wasteland and saluted the empty bowl with my weapon of choice. The satisfying gurgling sound of sludge disappearing down the pipes made my heart sing. Sad, really, that such a horrible affair could bring me so much satisfaction.

But when I spun to receive congratulations from my watcher, the adulation of my biggest fan, I found Petunia had rolled over on her side and went to sleep, her snoring lost until now in the slosh-slosh-slorp of my plunger.

"Typical." The orange top of my now beloved weapon settled into the white cup at the base of the toilet, squidging as it went. I'd have to make sure Mary cleaned it, at least. As for the throne itself, I sighed at the stench and the excess drips over the edge of the bowl and rather than fight with a seventy-year-old woman about boundaries, dug under the sink for cleaning supplies.

I knew which battles to pick. Fourteen long and educational days in and I'd learned more than I'd ever wanted to about the ins and outs of this new life of mine. Including just how very little the old lady was willing to do to make my life easier.

The bright yellow sponge didn't stay that color for long while I slopped cleaner into the now working throne and gave it a swipe with about as much enthusiasm as I'd approached this job from the beginning. If anyone had told me six months ago I'd be leaving New York City and my boyfriend of five years to come home to Reading, Vermont of all places, I'd have snorted my half-fat, 1/3 espresso, 2/3 regular, two pumps vanilla, one pump caramel whipped cream and chocolate sprinkles at them. Me and Curtis County at the foothills of the Green Mountains had said *sayonara* a decade ago as I scrambled my way out of small town blah and into the bright and shiny life of college and real life.

"And exactly how well did that work out for you, Fee Fleming?" I really needed my bangs cut, blowing them out of my way again with an impatient puff out of the corner of my mouth. But I'd paid two hundred bucks for my last trim and I doubted anyone in Reading could deliver.

Come to think of it, maybe there were perks.

Toilet bowl successfully cleaned, I leaned back on my haunches, sneakers squeaking on the tile, rubbing at my forehead with one arm and doing my best not to touch myself with unspeakable grossness. And found, to my surprise as I often did the last two weeks, despite the horrendousness of my existence at times, I actually felt good about being home. Happy, despite my cranky, melancholy staff, my fat pug adoptee, dirty toilets and fussy guests. Home had felt like the last place on Earth I'd ever find myself again and yet home was the best thing that had happened to me in a while.

"Just don't tell anyone I said so," I told Petunia who grunted and twitched in her sleep before starting to snore again.

A sniff of the air told me the cleaner had erased most of the stink of the regretful incident. A quick wipe with a towel and I was all set. Unsanitary? Yes, of course and I'd be sure to bleach the crap out of that same towel when I washed it. But I'd had enough of this entire mess and was ready to reemerge the victorious heroine of my own little story.

At least the guests would be happy.

Petunia farted so loudly she woke herself, sitting abruptly upright while the stench of her pug bowels surpassed anything I'd just managed to banish. And that moment that should have been mine, glory gained and earned, turned into a sorry state of affairs when Mary—bless her heart—poked her gray and judging head into the room, nose wrinkled as she took a sniff.

"You're wanted at the front desk," she said in her five packs a day though she didn't smoke voice before disappearing again.

I looked down at my brown bespeckled self and sighed. Of course I was.

CHAPTER TWO

I LEFT THE BATHROOM window wide open to the warmth of the July morning, already heating up despite the earliness of the hour. Air conditioning or not, the place needed some fresh breezes and a good smudging. I attempted a brave smile at the embarrassed older gentleman and his irritated wife, the current residents of the Carriage House's Blue Suite. Mr. and Mrs. Sprindle didn't comment much, though Mrs. Sprindle did take a minute to huff her robust self in half so she could pat Petunia on the head.

"Adorable," she said, pink in the cheeks with one hand clutching the front of her matching colored robe shut, rollers protruding from under her kerchief. Who wore rollers anymore? "I love pugs."

I didn't offer to send Petunia home with them. Barely. Instead, I left them to their morning, stepping out into the fresh air, exhaling in relief while I peeled away the stinky humidity of the yellow gloves. The sun rose over the mountains, beaming down on the extensive garden that separated the Carriage House (Blue Suite and Yellow Suite) from the main house (six more rooms of varying hues that were appropriately toned to match their names). The restored Colonial took up a double width lot compared to the rest of the street, camped on the end like a white-with-black-trim cap to the picturesque, tree lined small town residential neighborhood. Only a block from the boundaries deemed downtown and the quaint shops and tea rooms that popped up since local mayor, Olivia Walker, began her incessant drive to bring Reading into the present (using tourism to accomplish her implacable mission), Petunia's Bed and Breakfast was perfectly placed for a quiet and relaxing getaway at the foot of the Green Mountains.

Or had been. I paused in the early morning breeze, letting it blow the stink from my hair—yeah,

I chose to believe it was working—and drew a breath while the three giant koi in the carefully manicured pond in the middle of the garden rose to the surface of the still water to take turns touching their large, gaping lips to the pug's sniffing nose. Fat Benny, the biggest of the bunch, took the most time, but Pudgy Polly and Rotund Rudy had their turns, too.

Not my names, inherited from the old lady with a sense of humor. The best part? Petunia's. Yes, my grandmother, darling woman that she was, named her B&B after her dog. And not just this one. Oh, no. This particular incarnation of pugliness was the fourth.

Just sit with that for a second. Petunia the *Fourth*.

I shook my head and carried on, skirting the pond and the creepy orange fish Mary claimed my grandmother loved as much as her chubby canine. At least while the housekeeper and her sister, Betty, my cook, didn't seem to trust me just yet, Petunia herself had welcomed me with a charming and disconcerting attention that meant she followed me incessantly. Everywhere. All the time. Never, ever leaving me alone at all.

Teeth grind.

If only my ex had been so attentive I'd still be in New York. Then again, would I? I looked up at the towering mountains that felt enough like distant skyscrapers I wasn't uncomfortable, at the bright, blue sky and the trees with their spreading branches and mingling of oak and maple leaves and sighed. If I was going to be honest with myself, not something I'd been much in the past, I'd have to admit I hadn't been happy for a long time.

Petunia woofed softly, startling me, just as a piercing voice called my name. I knew before I even turned to look who stood at the fence between our properties, one skinny arm raised, hand flapping in greeting, beaming smile on her wrinkled face. Today, my neighbor Peggy Munroe wore a red bow in her hair, matching one holding the topknot of her creepily silent little dog in an upright flag of caramel fur that made her look like some kind of misshapen alien.

"Good morning, Fiona!" No matter how many times I told her to call me Fee, Peggy insisted on my full name. Because my grandmother did. Sigh. "Trouble in paradise, dear?"

I waved back, not in the mood to stop and chat endlessly with the nosy old woman. Who, I suspected, let her little dog skirt my fence and poop in my bushes. The soft piles of turds I'd uncovered were nowhere the size of Petunia's big deposits, but I didn't have proof so I left it alone. For now. "Busy busy as always, Peggy."

She shook her head, her bow bobbing as her little dog, Cookie, sneezed softly, delicately. "I have no idea what Olivia was thinking," she said, the same old song and dance conversation starting and exactly what I hoped to avoid. "Luring those developers to our little town, building that big resort and all." Yes, I'd heard this a million times before already, from her and from Mary and anyone else over the age of sixty-five who lived in Reading their whole lives. I could almost repeat what she was going to say next by rote, lips twitching in the need to mimic her as she went on. "Turned our dear little Reading into a cesspool of criminals and vagabonds."

"Tourists, you mean," I said softly, smiling.

She swatted the air in front of her, aimed at me, thin lips a tight line, faded blue eyes a match for her faintly tinted gray hair. "We were doing just fine before all her newfangled ideas." Did anyone actually talk like that anymore? Clearly Peggy Munroe did. And half the population of this town. Living in a valley surrounded by mountains had an effect on mental development, I guess. Amused, I let her go on, if only to grant me a bit of entertainment after the morning I'd had already and it wasn't even 8:30. "If it weren't for that Skip Anderson and the floozy he married…"

"I'm sure Willow Pink would be delighted to be called a floozy." Though Hollywood had called her worse. Still, she was an A-lister and her husband, said Skip, a famous football star. So I doubted they cared much through their veil of millions and hordes of fans what aging townsfolk naysayers—or the movie reviewers—thought of them.

Peggy snorted, not at all ladylike and reminding me of Petunia. "Well, if those two had the sense to keep our town out of the news like good Reading kids, we wouldn't be in this predicament."

True enough, at least. When Olivia asked Reading's most famous natives to join the tourism promotion team, they stepped up. And had they. Thanks to the new White Valley Ski Resort and Golf Club, Reading was suddenly a hub for tourists flocking to see the homestead of their favorite stars.

"Too late now." I grimaced at my watch. "Sorry, Peggy. I have to run."

"Ta-ta then, dear," she said, all cheerful again while Cookie watched me with what I always imagined to be a plea for mercy and rescue. "Come for tea soon, why don't you?"

I watched her blue-gray head of curls disappear behind the fence and not for the first time wondered what she found on her side to stand on so she could spy on my garden. Nosy neighbors. It took getting used to again.

Betty made her slow motion way around the kitchen as I entered through the back employee's door and crossed the tile floor. Head down, tight steely curls in a net that made her look like the crankiest cafeteria lady ever, the rounded bow to her wide back giving the Notre Dame lurker a run for his money, the other half of the Jones sisters ignored me as I intruded on her domain.

"Hi, Betty." I waved and smiled despite knowing she either didn't hear me or didn't care enough to acknowledge my presence. I'd never, in the fourteen days since arriving home and taking over Petunia's, heard the woman utter a single word. But she had heavy sighing down pat.

The portly pug at my side trotted over to her, abandoning me in favor of the bits of some kind of meat Betty was preparing, delivered from elevation into her gaping mouth. The whites of the pugs eyes showed as she scuttled her butt from side to side, barely able to contain herself.

"Bye, Betty." I left the faithless dog to her snack, knowing she'd likely get sick later from the excess and that I'd be the one forced to clean it up. But it freed me from her constant plodding attention for the time being.

Kind of insulting, really, she chose food over me every single time.

I really should have taken the effort to scoot downstairs to my apartment and clean up, but as I considered the prospect of meeting whoever waited for me without a skim of fecal matter between us I spotted trouble at the end of the hallway, right at the tall, bright front entry.

Her chatter reached me first, though not the words themselves. It was the tone, the sparkling and overly cheerful, if genuine, rapid fire energy expelling itself from the flapping mouth of my old bestie that drove me down the hall at a clip, past Mary who muttered under her breath about the dirt on my sneakers. Well, she could just do her job and vacuum once in a while. Not my fault the B&B went from sedate one or two bookings a week to over packed and bursting at the seams since the shining lights of Reading sang their siren call to all the good people of the world to come visit now, you hear?

Daisy Bruce, eternal teenage optimist despite our matching chronological ages, turned as I joined her, beaming at me so brightly I longed for a pair of sunglasses to cut the brilliance. Okay, so poor Day. I was, admittedly, a bit grumpy this morning, but could anyone blame me, really? And the towering, broad figure who loomed over my old friend's slim blondeness wasn't making me feel like my fortunes had turned.

If anything, the red faced man who might have been a football linebacker in a former decade but had gone too far to beer and burgers for his own good had that kind of expression on his thick lipped face that made me want to back up a step and reassess the situation. His beady blue eyes, so pale they were almost transparent, squinted out of folds, his faintly reddish hair, what was left of it, combed over the shining top of his head. And he had that bully stance, the kind that big men with little care for women seemed to think would make me back down if they just waited long enough.

I lived in New York for five years. We'd just see who backed down first.

"Oh, Fee," Daisy gushed, grasping my upper arm with both hands as if she had no idea she was transferring unmentionable fluids from myself to her. Her pale gray eyes gleamed with charm and not a whole lot else while she grinned first at me then up at the large man in the jeans and shining silver belt buckle, whose plaid shirt stretched over the round of his protruding belly. Cowboy boots crushed the deep blue carpet beneath him, pointed toes decorated with chrome. "You're here, at last." Daisy rolled her eyes and giggled. "I told you she'd be right here, silly." She released me long enough to playfully slap the man's forearm, coyness not an act.

"Fiona Fleming?" He smiled, too, but my stomach turned when he did, an oily tone to his deep voice.

I nodded. "Can I help you? Mr…?"

Instead of gracing me with his own name, he extended one big hand toward me. How had I missed the large envelope he held pressed to one leg? I took it out of reflex, confused as I looked down at my name printed on an official looking label in the center. I glanced up to find him turning to leave without even so much as a hint of explanation.

"Excuse me," I said, the envelope outstretched toward him as if doing so would grant me some kind of insight. "What is this?"

"Deed papers," he said, grinning now. "Thanks to your grandmother's dying signature, Petunia's belongs to me."

I gaped at him, frozen in place, and watched in growing horror while the big, white door slammed shut behind him.

CHAPTER THREE

MY ASTONISHED AND PARALYZED state didn't last long and before I knew I was in motion I found myself jerking open the entry and hurtling down the front steps to the flagstone walk. Even so, the man's long stride had carried him a great distance and I only caught up as he was climbing into a giant monstrosity of a black SUV. I nabbed his arm, pulling him toward me, though honestly he was twice my size at least and had he wanted to just leave, there wasn't much I could do to stop him. But he did pause, still grinning, handing me a business card.

"When you're ready to hand over the keys," he said, "next day or two would be good for me, I'll be waiting for your call."

"There's obviously some mistake." My brain fired, spun, wobbled on its axis. This was nuts. My grandmother left Petunia's to me. Why would she sign it over to some stranger? I glanced down at the card in my hand. Pete Wilkins, Wilkins Construction, Inc. Did I even know him from growing up here? "You've obviously got the wrong place."

"If you're any longer than forty-eight hours," he said as if I hadn't even spoken, "I'll make sure the sheriff comes along when I take possession." He snickered at that. Like this was funny. "To give you encouragement to move out."

Move… "I'm not going anywhere." Heat washed over me that had nothing to do with the growing temperature of the day, the sun overhead, the July humidity. Now, I'm not saying I have a bad temper, but, well. I *am* a redhead. Scare me or push me or corner me? Ka-boom. I waved the envelope at him as he climbed into his truck with a grunt, slamming the door. "You'll be hearing from my lawyer." Because I had a lawyer. Yikes.

Pete Wilkins leaned out the open window, saluting me with two fingers. "Have a nice day, Miss Fleming," he said before laughing and keying a button, the whir of rising tinted glass cutting me off.

"Get back here right now!" Oh my god, did I really just stomp my foot on the sidewalk like a little kid having a tantrum? He backed into the street as if he owned it, squealing his tires when he drove off while I shook and shouted at his retreating license plate. "I want an explanation for this!"

"Fee?" Daisy's soft and worried tone didn't help at all. If anything, her timidity made things worse. I spun on her, spotted a pair of guests staring, Peggy Munroe observing from her front door. Confrontation was a spectator sport in Reading, was that it? "Is everything okay?"

She will never know how much inner strength and fortitude it took not to smack her with the damned envelope I clutched so tightly in my hand my fingers were tingling. She did have the good sense to back up a pace, though, and my guests, suitcases in hand, hurried inside as if I might blow at any moment. As for Peggy, she didn't comment, she and Cookie going inside as if disappointed there wouldn't be fireworks.

As for me, I inhaled. Exhaled. And dropped Pete Wilkins's card on the sidewalk before carefully and precisely shredding it under my sneaker.

"We have guests," I said abruptly to Daisy and stomped back inside.

Thursday was turnover heavy, one of my busiest days, and instead of being able to take my time and peruse the clearly mistaken document that remained hidden inside the large envelope, I instead shoved it into a drawer at the sideboard that housed the computer in the foyer and got back to work.

Cleaning and check-ins and a long, weary day later and I realized I hadn't had a chance to even change out of the stinky clothes I'd worn to clean the toilet in the Blue Suite. With a last sigh of disgust at myself, stomach growling from lack of dinner, I finally paused in the front hall near the desk and removed the envelope. Looked up around the beautifully decorated front entry with its delightful crystal light fixtures and vaulted ceiling, the bright, white wooden slats and soft blue walls. My grandmother's taste had been impeccable, to say the least. There was nothing old fashioned or creepy about Petunia's. In fact, I loved it, more than I'd care to admit, even after this short time as the mistress of this place.

If these papers were legit, how was I going to bear giving up this life I thought would rescue me from myself?

"It's going to be okay, Fee," Daisy said, coming to my side, voice still soft and apologetic. "Won't it?"

I had a very, very bad feeling it wasn't. But the initial burn of fury was gone, leaving behind the kind of sick knotting that usually led to me making terrible life choices. "Sure it will," I said. "Can you handle things here for a bit?"

Bless her, she didn't do a whole lot, really not suited to working for me on the physical, manual labor side. But I didn't have the heart to fire her—considering I hadn't officially hired her in the first place—when she'd bustled back into my life like an excited kid whose favorite toy had been found after long absence. And she really was good with the guests. Like Petunia, they treated her as if her adorableness was endearing so I shrugged off her lack of focus and ability in the bed making and bathroom cleaning department and let her handle the desk.

"Of course," she gushed. "You can count on me." She saluted, cute little flowered sundress as flawless as when she'd arrived this morning, perfectly polished nails unchipped. And while leaving her in charge likely meant a disaster waiting to happen, I had to face this ridiculous prospect I might not really own Petunia's after all.

With the envelope clutched in my hand and the waddling pug on a leash at my side, I strode out of the front door and down the street at a smart clip. My temper pushed me faster and faster, only to hear the chuffing puffs of protest that spun me around. Petunia now strolled behind me—way behind me—her short legs plodding under her round body, tongue hanging at a comical angle, corkscrew tail wagging its jolly best as she tried to keep up. The harness around her chest sat askew, retractable leash at its maximum reach.

"You could have stayed home." Annoyance at her helped cut the edge of my worry as Petunia finally joined me and sat on her haunches, back legs tucked sideways under her as if she planned to stay a while. She grumbled a few pug things at me, ending in a soft growling bark that told me exactly what she thought of me leaving her behind.

"Fine," I said, spinning and marching on, though at a pace more suited to Petunia this time. "But don't you dare tell Mom you missed dinner. I know Betty gave you seconds."

The pug burped softly before farting with great enthusiasm.

Almost enough to make me smile.

I rounded the end of the block and past a short, white picket fence, the familiar sight of my father's pickup truck and Mom's cute little custom pink Volkswagen Beetle crowding their narrow driveway. At least they were both home. I was going to need the two of them on this, I had a feeling, even if just to commiserate on my loss if it came to that.

I wasn't expecting the sight of the big, white sheriff's truck parked across the street, nor of the tall, broad shouldered and white hatted uniform who strode out the front door of my parent's rancher with a tip of his brim, boots thudding on the patio stones as he sauntered down the walk as if he knew just how freaking delicious he looked 24/7.

Sheriff Crew Turner paused at the gate, grinning at Petunia who he bent to give a good scratch behind one ear before he squinted up at me, blue eyes narrowed against the sun setting behind the mountains. It gave him a rugged appearance, like he'd strode out of a cowboy movie though I knew for a fact he was from southern California and not somewhere as cliché as Wyoming or Texas.

"Miss Fleming." He'd yet to call me Fee, and while we'd only met once, in passing, a week ago when he took over as county sheriff from my dad, I figured first name basis was a good place to start.

"Just Fee," I said. "Sheriff."

He stood, frowning slightly, eyes catching the envelope, my obvious upset. Because I'd never been able to hide it when I was ready to lose my mind, uh-huh. The whole world knew when Fiona Fleming was pissed. "Problem?"

"Personal." I really should have tried harder with him, considering there weren't many manly options around here, but it had been a hell of a day. As much as I would have loved to flirt and maybe do something about that handsomeness that involved wine and dinner, not only was I in a terrible mood, surely I still stank, even after all the hours I'd put between me and the carriage house toilet incident.

Crew glanced back over his shoulder and I followed his gaze, to find my father, just as tall and wide through the shoulders, really a carbon copy of the new sheriff if three decades older, glaring at the two of us like having a conversation was against the law. Dad chose to retire, so it wasn't like he resented Crew for taking his job. Or maybe he did?

"Nice to see you again, Miss… Fee." Crew tipped his hat, black hair falling over his eyes before smiling down at the panting pug. "Madam Petunia." And then he walked away and I wished I didn't have this crap to deal with so I could find out if it was just the cut of his jeans that made his butt look so damned fine.

What? I was due some distraction, thank you.

With a heavy heart and a terrible feeling, I plodded to the door and looked up at my dad.

"I think I'm in trouble," I said. And handed him the unopened envelope.

CHAPTER FOUR

MOM WAS AT THE kitchen sink when Dad led the way through the front door and to the back of the house. I loved their open concept with the vaulted ceilings and newly renovated clean lines. Dad had always seemed content with the seventies-esque feel of the place, but it was nice to see my mother finally got her way when Dad decided it might be time to think about retirement.

"I honestly believe he didn't want to spend every day home hearing me complain about the cabinets and carpeting," she admitted in a girly giggle that made me smile just a week ago over coffee.

My socks skidded on the newly polished hardwood floors as I scuffed my feet on my way through to the marble tiles that glowed in the sunlight, the slab of granite Mom chose a hulking monstrosity on the surface of the large island she decided on for the centerpiece of the new kitchen. The last of the sunbeams poured in the sliding glass doors, lighting the room in a heavenly glow that instantly made me feel better. I sighed as I hugged Mom, her cheek against mine, matching auburn hair without a hint of gray, though I knew she had a box to thank for that. Still, her lack of wrinkles and constant cheery expression gave me hope I'd age gracefully.

Either that or I'd end up like my mountain of a Dad with a permanently grouchy look on my face. I'd pick Mom's sunny optimism any day. Too bad it didn't pick me back.

"Sweetie!" Mom spun toward the counter and the glass enclosed sculpture of chocolate standing on a charming pedestal. She swept the cover free, gesturing to the untouched cake that lured me like the call of a distant siren. "I just finished frosting it. Want a slice?" She didn't wait for an affirmation, carving out a gigantic piece from the three tiered deliciousness while the scent of cocoa and way too much sugar wafted toward me thanks to the slowly revolving white fan blades turning in lazy relief of the heat over my head. Great reminder I hadn't eaten and probably not the best choice on an empty stomach. But eggs, flour, milk—food groups, right? And worth the sore tummy and the inevitable sugar crash.

"Thanks, Mom," I said. "I could use a little TLC after the day I've had."

She paused to share a sad face. "I wish you'd just let me help you at the house," she said. "I'm happy to do it, Fee."

"You have earned your retirement," I shook my head as I leaned on the counter, body tired now that I'd stopped for a minute. "And I should be able to handle one bed and breakfast. Right?" My mouth watered while I accepted the plate from her, the idea of the chocolatey deliciousness almost more than I could stand.

"You know how much I love to cook," she said. "I'm dying to try some new recipes. You could expand, offer lunch."

I hesitated with a bite of cake near my lips. "Would you fire Betty for me?"

Mom flinched then laughed, blushing. "Listen to me, being so rude. Of course not. Betty and Mary have been with Iris and Petunia's for simply ages." She looked down at the hopeful pug sitting at her feet, the whites of her bulging eyes showing as if anticipating a treat. "Hasn't she, good girl?"

Petunia whined softly and licked her lips.

"Don't even think about it." I waved my fork at Mom who seemed to be considering the unthinkable. "The pug doesn't get sugar." Or chocolate. All I needed was my grandmother to come back to haunt me because I poisoned her precious Petunia.

Dad grunted, opening the envelope as he raised one bushy gray eyebrow at her. "Sure, Fee gets offered," he said, sounding much more grumpy than he really was. I knew from experience how much he loved teasing his beloved wife. "And the damned dog. But I want some? Forget it."

"You," she spun and tapped him on the back of one hand with the spatula, dotting frosting on his skin, "are on a diet." She tossed her full head of hair and winked at me, even as she ladled a second piece onto a plate, just as big as the first, followed by a more modest one for herself.

Ah, the parent dance. It hadn't changed one bit since I was a kid. So predictably sweet and endearing. And made me feel almost instantly like I was ten again. Not necessarily the best reaction when I had very grown up things to worry about. But it was nice to perch on the soft seat of the stool at the island and take a big, heavenly bite of Mom's prized chocolate cake and let my father read over the paperwork that dread had kept me from opening myself.

Sure, I was a big girl now. But that didn't mean I couldn't find support and love from the two people who brought me into the world while cold milk and cake healed the hurt in my heart.

Dad didn't touch his dessert, starting to swear softly under his breath, eyebrows meeting in the middle while his cheeks turned first pink then dark red. The tendons in his neck stood out in impressive ropes and I only then wondered if I'd made a huge mistake not breaking this whole mess to him more gently. After all, it was his mother who supposedly signed away the B&B, right? While dying from the deterioration brought on by a debilitating stroke in a nursing home. I really was an idiot.

Mom leaned in, one hand on his wrist, concerned expression making me feel worse. I swallowed hastily and spoke up as Dad continued to read and mutter swearwords that made me wince.

"Supposedly," I said, looking back and forth between them, "Grandmother Iris signed paperwork that deeded Petunia's to some guy named Pete Wilkins." Mom hissed a sharp intake of breath, green eyes flashing to Dad who crumpled the papers in one giant hand and tossed them to the marble countertop.

"We'll just see about that." And then he stormed out like a marching juggernaut on his way to do damage. I gaped after him and his sudden departure, cake forgotten.

"Oh, dear," Mom sighed, staring down at her own slice. "This is terrible."

"You're not kidding," I said. "Could it be real?" This was the first time I actually allowed myself to accept fully it might be, absolutely, and that my whole reason for coming home was about to fall out from under me. A gaping maw of panic rose up inside me, choking my breath. What would I do? Where would I go? I couldn't, at almost twenty-nine, move back in with my parents. Wouldn't. But returning to New York? That was impossible now.

I'd burned that bridge. Dear God, what was I going to do?

Mom must have known my head was spinning because she scooted around the island and took the stool Dad vacated, leaning in to hug me before carefully smoothing out the wrinkles and then perusing the paper he'd discarded. Her years as an English teacher might not have made her a lawyer, but she taught Law, too, so she at least would know something, right?

She finally slipped the offending sheets, still wonky from Dad's furious attention, back into the envelope and set them before her, little hands folding over the surface, covering my name with those familiar fingers. My eyes settled on the ridges of skin that were the proof of years of contentment cupping the wedding band and engagement ring she'd worn since she was eighteen. Coral polish shone on her perfectly oval nails, faintly blue veins showing under the thinning skin. Weird how those details came into sharp focus for me at a time like this, but I found the longer I stared at those hands I knew so well, hands I'd missed being away from this long, the deeper I was able to breathe and the more my rational thoughts returned, banishing the panic until I was able to concentrate when Mom spoke.

"John will blame himself for this," she said, tears in her eyes. "There's old, bad blood between him and Pete, Fee. And it has nothing to do with you, or Iris. So sad." Mom shook her head, stared down into Dad's untouched cake. "But don't worry a bit, all right? Your father will get this sorted. There's not a single thing to fuss over." She grasped and squeezed my hand, forced a brave little smile. "Okay, sweetie? Not a single thing."

That routine worked when I was a kid. But I wasn't so sure Mom's goodness and light was going to come to the rescue this time. Not that I didn't appreciate the effort.

"What bad blood?" I reached for the envelope, hating the thing now though I personally hadn't looked at the contents and it was just paper and ink. Soulless, impersonal. Not worthy of hate, really.

Mom sniffled and stood, taking Dad's plate, replacing carefully the slice of uneaten cake on the glass pedestal, doing the same with her own, before setting the cover softly on the base. "It doesn't matter now," she said. "John's retired. It's Crew Turner's problem from here."

So this was a criminal matter turned personal? "Mom," I said. "I'd better call a lawyer."

She turned and smiled again, not quite so fake anymore. "Just let your father talk to Pete," she said. "I'm sure he'll get it all sorted out." She hesitated before her chin dropped a little, brave face fading. "You have his mind, his passion for truth. I wish…"

I didn't want to talk about Dad's insistence I not follow in his footsteps, the only thing I'd ever really wanted. Too depressing.

Mom must have agreed. "Eat your cake, Fee."

And while it was probably the last thing I wanted to do now, I did as I was told like a good girl. By the time I was done, Mom standing in contemplative silence in the slowly darkening kitchen so long my last few bites were like eating in the most uncomfortable quiet of my entire life, I had to choke down the final swallow. When I rose to take the plate and fork to the sink, turning on the light under the counters to cut the shadows, she jerked into motion again, her beaming smile firmly in place, Petunia snuffling at her feet as a few crumbs fell when Mom scooped the dishes out of my hands.

"Now, don't forget, six o'clock Saturday," she said, depositing the plate and fork into the sink before turning me and aiming me for the front door. So, time to go then, was it? I grabbed the envelope, Petunia trailing mournfully after me. "Dinner for my birthday. You won't forget?"

She sounded worried. I turned and hugged her. "I wish you'd let us take you out. Or at least allow me to cook for you."

Mom beamed then, kissing my cheek, bending to pat Petunia's wrinkled head. "The very best gift I can receive is to cook whatever I want for my own birthday." She nodded sharply once with a gleam in her eyes. "I can't wait."

Petunia grunted while Mom ushered us smoothly out the door and waved. I gave up trying to argue, impressed as always at how deft she seemed to be, the effortless way she managed to shoo me along, and finished sliding my heels into my sneakers before heading for home.

The second my feet hit the sidewalk, street lights flickering to life despite the fact on the other side of the mountains the sun still shone, a horrible thought struck me. I really was going to need a lawyer. And I knew a good one, a damned good one with tons of experience and enough motivation to represent me for free I'd likely win no matter what kind of paperwork Pete Wilkins thought he had against me.

The only trouble was that lawyer was my ex. And I just wasn't willing to go there.

Sighing over the Pandora's box of my history and hoping Mom's attempt at reassurance meant I could keep Ryan Richards safely in the past, I slumped my way home to the B&B while the namesake of that same place grunted and snorted and farted beside me.

CHAPTER FIVE

THIS TIME, THE WALK wasn't fueled by anger, and rather than forcing myself to stroll I took my time easily. Settling into Petunia's waddling pace gave me the minutes I needed to sort out my head so when I at last set foot on the bottom step of the B&B's front entry, any plans to make a hasty call to New York and the guy I'd left behind were firmly and completely squashed flat and forced into a tiny compartment of nope in the back of my mind reserved for idiot decisions that never saw the light of day.

Big girl, here.

I bent and scratched Petunia's ears, making her groan in delight, her bulging eyes closing as she leaned into my hands. "Thanks for the company," I said, kissing the top of her wrinkled brow. "We'll get this sorted, pug. Won't we?"

She snorted in my face before lolling out her tongue like she was laughing at me, cinnamon bun tail wriggling. A face only a pug lover could adore and I guess I was turning into one.

I wasn't even in the front door when I heard Daisy's raised voice, grateful to have her here despite her bumbling at times, just so I could have some time outside these walls. Really not in the mood for people but not having a choice, I plastered on a smile and greeted my late arriving guests while my old bestie beamed at me like she hadn't been working all day already.

If only I could be that kind of charismatic extrovert. I think I'd choke myself.

Daisy sent off for the evening and the Jones sisters long since departed at their appointed hour, I was on my own the rest of the evening, a giant jigsaw puzzle of guests, putting out fires—figurative and literal when Petunia knocked over a candle someone left burning—and general business that tended to drop me onto my private couch in the basement apartment by 9PM every night. And though it was taking some getting used to, I wasn't complaining.

I should have been. Being home raised a lot of old stuff, my desire to pursue law enforcement crushed by Dad not the very least of my ancient aches. Mom had to bring it up, didn't she? And seeing Crew in that uniform, well. It wasn't just his well-formed behind in those jeans that made me sigh. Those could have been *my* jeans.

Okay, that didn't exactly come out right. "You'll forgive my line of thinking," I said to Petunia, amused by her head tilt and giant eyes as she quickly licked her lips of the last of her evening snack in silent plea for more food. "What I meant to say was if things were different, if I'd ignored Dad and gone for it, would I be in Crew's place right now?" At Crew's place, candle light, bottle of wine…

This was just too confusing, even for me.

I fell into bed a short time later, mind spinning with minutia as if to distract me from the real issue that loomed over my head. The paperwork I still hadn't looked too closely at, the envelope lurking in my kitchen, left there to haunt me as if it could sprout legs and ease its nasty self into my bedroom, slip up onto the comforter and smother me in malicious glee in the middle of the night.

It didn't help Petunia peered over the edge of the bed at me, those soulful eyes begging for an invitation. The padded, carpeted staircase my grandmother had left at the foot of the bed for her beloved pug had been immediately relocated to the closet night one together, about the same time Petunia thought my pillow was an ideal place to nap.

"Sorry, pug," I said, firmly closing my eyes to her desperate cuteness. "You have a perfectly good bed on the floor. I suggest you get used to it." Because I didn't share. Except maybe with the right man in uniform…

Oh, Fee.

Petunia sighed and stared.

"Well, what do you think I should do?" I couldn't help but think about Ryan and the warm spot that used to be full of him. Back when I had no idea he was a cheating ass who had no regard for the fact I'd put his sorry butt through law school as a barista/waitress/office assistant/anything I could work at that would pay me while still sucking out my soul. Not his fault, I guess, I could never decide what

I wanted to be for the rest of my life. But the cheating? On his conscience.

I was still trying to figure out my own path even now, though the idea I could turn into my grandmother, spend the rest of my life running this place, didn't sound so bad, despite my old need to escape Reading's tiny, judging clutches. "Do I call him or not?"

The pug chuffed softly, ending in a whining yawn.

"You're right," I said, turning over, punching my pillow with vigor and determination. "We can handle it, can't we? Best to let that particular dog lie." I looked up, winced at her scrunched expression. "No offense intended."

Another chuff and a deeper sigh. She finally turned and sank to the floor, ignoring the expensive bed I'd gone out and acquired for her so I didn't have to feel guilty not letting her sleep with me. Because I didn't feel badly she spent her every night with my grandmother on this very bed but had been doomed to an existence on the cold, hard floor for the rest of her life because I was selfish.

At least, that's what I imagined she was thinking. Not me. Nope. No guilt here.

I faded out to the sound of her high-pitched barking as she chased something in her sleep.

I woke briefly, disoriented and cotton mouthed, blearily raising my head, eyes settling on the clock next to my bed. 2:34, far too early to be getting up just yet. What prodded me awake? Only then did I see Petunia standing next to the bed, staring up at me. The whites of her eyes showed, gleaming in the low light of the clock's red glow. Refusing to be freaked out by the demonic appearance of my grandmother's portly pug, I turned over, snuggling my pillow again even as Petunia woofed once, softly and questioningly, before I fell into deep slumber again.

Surely 5:45 was early enough to catch the two Jones sisters not yet at their posts. I'd added an extra five minutes each morning the past two weeks just to see if I could catch them before they arrived. But sneaking up the back stairs to the kitchen proved my attempt to win this particular battle was foiled again.

There they were, both of them. Looking about as perky as they ever did. Standing by the stove, drinking coffee like they'd been here for hours. I knew they both left. I watched them go each evening—if missing their departure last night—at precisely 5 o'clock like they had things to attend to and not a second later. Maybe they both snuck back in the middle of the night and slept in a closet just so they could beat me to the kitchen every damned time?

I forced a smile on and entered like I owned the place. Which was in question, wasn't it? "Good morning, ladies." At least I sounded chipper if I didn't feel it.

Petunia bypassed me, huffing toward the back door and the garden to do her business. I held the screen open for her while the sisters in dourness stared at me over the rims of their mugs.

"Miss Fleming," Mary said for both of them. Just like every other morning. The corner of my right eye twitched and I suddenly wondered if they were the cause of my grandmother's death. Their relentless humdrumness finally killed her and would be the end of me, too, wouldn't it? I had a horrible, lurking terror in that moment I'd wake up twenty years from now with the doldrum sisters, wrinkled and shaking, still staring at me like they'd never, ever accept me.

Coffee would save me. I lunged for the pot only to have Betty hand me a cup. I knew before I sipped it not only was it still hot, but perfectly flavored to my exact specifications. Which just made me want to throw it in the sink and drink tea.

"Thanks," I said, trying to sound like I meant it.

"Funny she's barking." Mary nodded to silent Betty. "She never barks."

I glanced at the back door, freezing in place. I'd missed it in my descent into irritated misery, the sound of Petunia through the kitchen door. They were right. Curiosity lured me, drew me out into the garden, following the path and the sound of her puggy protesting. The old English garden feel made the place a bit of a maze at times. I circled the pond and the towering grasses waving in the breeze and froze as the view cleared, my eyes and brain having a bit of a cha-cha for a moment while someone screamed.

I'm pretty sure it wasn't me.

Nope, not me. Mrs. Sprindle, in fact, her pink slippers wet at the toes as she stared down into the water, the trio of fat, orange fish poking the swollen, staring face of Pete Wilkins beneath the surface. A thin stream of blood flowed from beneath his thin hair like a flag of crimson that slowly faded away as the water diffused it.

The very man I wished would burn in hell for all eternity. Dead. In my koi pond.

Was it wrong I instantly wondered what this meant for his claim on Petunia's? And that the look on the now silent pug's face as she panted and squatted nearby gave me the impression she was delighted with this turn of events?

CHAPTER SIX

IN A NORMAL, WELL-ADJUSTED and orderly world, Petunia's would have been shut down in about a heartbeat, the place swarmed with cops, my week of income ruined and a plethora of furious and frustrated guests hammering me with their unhappiness with the fact my bed and breakfast was no longer available for their vacationing needs.

But this was Reading, Vermont. And I hadn't forgotten just how little this town I grew up in followed anything resembling ordinary.

About three seconds after my morning-addled mind processed the dead guy in my water feature, another two or so seconds following the end of Mrs. Sprindle's echoing shriek that told me she likely had a history in theater or professional music, and maybe about a heartbeat before I could draw a breath and utter the horrible thought out loud this was probably the best way my morning could have gone, Mary's graveled voice echoed toward me from the kitchen door.

"Better call the sheriff," she said. Dear God, did she actually sound bored?

I stumbled to the main house and dialed the requisite 9-1-1 before collapsing onto a stool and hugging myself briefly, a chill passing over my entire body though the morning was already warm. How long I sat there I have no idea, except the first thing to shake me out of my guilty near hysteria that the man who wanted to take Petunia's from me was now all kinds of dead wasn't a deputy or the sheriff or even my dad.

No. The firm hand on my arm with the crisp, nude nail polish and the tasteful diamond ring squeezed with the kind of attention one attributed to a politician. I looked up, dazed, lost, into the professionally concerned and yet kind face of Mayor Olivia Walker.

"Darling Fiona," she said, guiding me to my feet with her continuing grip on my elbow. We'd met once, so when I became her darling I have no idea. It was nice to have the comfort, though. I staggered upright, nodded to her, gulped. "Are you all right?"

Considering there was a dead man in my koi pond and, now that I thought about it, I was probably a suspect, wasn't I? Yeah, not so all right.

"What are you doing here?" Not that I meant to be rude, but you can imagine my confusion. I'd called the police, not the middle-aged, pant suited and perfectly put together leader of our fair little town.

She didn't seem to take the question personally, kind smile refusing to quit past her precise lip liner. "I was in the sheriff's office when the call came in, my dear," she said. Finally released my arm and patted my shoulder with efficiency and charm that only made my confusion worse. "I'm here for you in this terrible time."

"I didn't know you were a lawyer." I stared mournfully at the deputies and paramedics who, I now noticed, trundled past, nodding to me or ignoring me on their way by.

"You won't be needing a lawyer, Fiona," Olivia said with a crisp kind of command that perked me up despite my disorientation. Petunia grumbled a bit and only then did I notice she'd come to sit at my feet, watching with her black ears cocked. “Petunia’s is a valuable addition to this town’s tourism economy and I will not see you closed down for one instant. No matter the circumstances.”

She *what*? I gaped while Olivia half turned and nodded brusquely to Crew who came to a halt next to us. I could barely meet his eyes, breath held so long black spots danced in my vision while he scowled down at her like I wasn’t even there.

“Police procedure,” he said through gritted teeth. “I can’t have guests trampling the crime scene.”

“And I won’t have you sully the good name of this bed and breakfast or its host in the eyes of the world.” I shook my head as Olivia tucked one arm through mine, her pale yellow suit jacket making my skin look sallow. I just didn’t have her olive complexion, black hair or dark brown eyes. It worked really well for her, though. And clearly I’d lost my mind because instead of worrying about the dead dude I was comparing skin tones and color combinations.

Marvelous start to a Friday. Well, at least I wasn’t plunging a toilet. Yet.

“Madam Mayor,” Crew said, still completely ignoring me, his brow pulled into lines over his eyes, tan doing nothing to hide the redness of his face as his temper visibly grew. Damn, he was cute when he was pissed. "You do realize a man has died here."

"A most unfortunate event." The mayor tugged me closer, shaking her head and tsking her sympathy. "Was he a tourist?" That was the first time she seemed even remotely worried for real.

"No," I managed. "Local."

Crew scowled at me at last while Olivia's faint, sympathetic smile returned, grip all the tighter on my arm. "Well, then I'm sure you'll agree, Sheriff, any local would want our economy to thrive and grow, not be affected by their passing. Especially considering this is a big weekend for Reading and the lodge is full to capacity."

I couldn't believe what I was hearing but was in no position to fight her. Not while a mix of shock and still threatening hysterical laughter bubbled in my stomach and threatened to spin me to the big sink where I could noisily throw up everything I'd ever eaten. Ever.

"You don't get to dictate—"

Olivia's smile slipped as she leaned in to the still protesting Crew.

"You clean this up," she hissed, all pretense gone, "and get that body out of here before the whole town sees it. And Petunia's stays open. I mean it, Crew. You think I've been a hard ass since you took over? Think that parking dispute was any indication of how far I'll go?" Um, what? "You haven't seen anything yet." She jerked on my arm slightly before seeming to realize what she'd done. Olivia's dark brown eyes caught mine, not a trace of caring there. But she did care, at least for this town, and if her being a pit bull about tourism meant I stayed open…

Crew knew he'd lost from the look of utter fury on his face. Again his eyes flickered to me. Did he blame me for this? Instead of commenting, he pushed past both of us, bellowing orders I barely caught as I sagged into the stool again while Olivia brushed at the front of her jacket.

"You have an instant of trouble from that young man," she said, "and you call my office immediately."

CHAPTER SEVEN

SHE LEFT ME THERE, her previously unseen assistant hurrying after her, the petite young man in the precision suit that could have been from New York waving to me on the way by. I'd never even met him, but I waved back anyway.

Did she control the media, too, our mayor? I could only believe that was the case because as the next hour unfurled with lengths of yellow police tape and a firm and unhappy speech from Crew to my guests about staying behind the line while the whispering gathering snapped photos of Pete Wilkins's sheet covered body being wheeled out of my garden, not one reporter made an appearance.

Well, Reading only had one reporter. But still.

I stood off to one side as the bulk of the deputies left. By bulk, I mean two, leaving Robert Carlisle behind. My first cousin wasn't my favorite person in the whole world—we'd spent enough rivalry energy as kids trying to make each other kiss dirt to really get along—and the fact he'd decided to pursue the career I'd always longed for didn't endear him to me any.

Especially because he told me at high school graduation the only reason he was going to the academy was because I couldn't. Jerk.

Rather than engage him in any kind of attempt to pretend I was civil right now, I stayed out of the way, unable to stop myself, however, from lingering near the police tape, staring into the pond where the three fat koi swam, a mix of horror and relief so at odds I was sure I was going to explode. So wrong to be grateful the hideous man was dead. And yet he was *dead*. On *my property*. What was he doing here? And when did he die? I'd poked around enough in forensics out of curiosity over the years it was pretty obvious he hadn't been there long. A few hours? And what was that odd, round impression in the dirt next to the rock border of the pond? Not very big—about the circumference of the top of an old fashioned glass ketchup bottle and maybe an inch deep—but pretty obvious. Looked ridged, a near perfect mirror image to whatever left it there. Impossible to miss, really. Did the deputies photograph it? I had to clench my hands on my biceps to keep from moving closer to look.

Okay, I might end up a suspect, but I didn't kill him, so it was all good. And while the immediate issue was out of the way, he had to have heirs. Did that mean whoever inherited from him owned Petunia's? Was it even a valid claim now? Who did I track down and shake really hard to find out?

Hey, was that blood on that rock? I'd seen a faint trail of it in the water coming from the back of Pete's head. Did it mean he'd slipped and fallen, that his death was an accident? Hang on, there was more blood. No, wait. Something red, though, dangling from Fat Benny's gross fishy lips.

"Robert." I really didn't want to talk to him but someone needed to know. "I think they missed something."

I pointed at the scrap of what looked like cloth, grimaced when my cousin leaned in around me, thumbs tucked in his belt and grinned past his ridiculous black mustache that made him look like a refugee from the 70's disco scene.

"You cracked the case, Fanny," he said. "Guess we'll have to take the fish in for questioning."

His guffawing laughter echoed back and forth between the main and carriage house as if to prove to me he was funny. The hated nickname he'd used against me like a weapon since we were five years old reverberated in my brain, setting off firework explosions of rage that likely did permanent damage. His attempt to rile me up as a kid with the obvious reference to my butt had turned into a sly maliciousness he'd never grown out of. I really needed to get out of there. I couldn't keep my mind on one track for long. Punching Robert in the nose was probably not a great choice at this point. And looking back at the crime scene did me no favors. Not when it seemed like the long, smooth scuff at the base of the pond could have been the mark of an expensive boot sliding on the mud.

"Miss Fleming." I spun with a bit of a shriek, hands flying to cover my mouth, hating that I'd been caught not only snooping—I hadn't realized I'd come to the edge of the police tape and was leaning in to look at the crime scene—but sounded guilty about it. About a lot of things. The sheriff didn't look very understanding, either.

"Sorry." I backed up and leaped to one side when Petunia yelped, bent to massage her paw in apology for her, too. This morning needed to be over.

"I don't appreciate being told how to run my crime scene, Miss Fleming." Crew crossed his arms over his chest and clenched his jaw. So much for calling me Fee. "While I realize it's not your fault,"—why did he sound like that was questionable?—"I'll be leaving a deputy here to enforce the security of the scene. Just in case."

I nodded quickly. "Anything I can do, Sheriff."

His scowl didn't lighten. "I think you've done enough." That stink eye look. What the hell did that mean exactly? He just admitted the whole Olivia thing wasn't on me. Tell me handsome and jerk didn't go hand in hand in this case. Though, I had to admit, I was grateful for his attitude because it snapped me out of the fugue of weirdness and shock that had held me all morning.

"Was it an accident?" I gestured behind me. "Looks like blood on the rock. There was more in the water. Slip marks in the mud could be from a man's shoe." Or smooth bottomed cowboy boot.

When I turned back, Crew's eyes had narrowed so far I wished I'd kept my mouth shut.

"Don't mind my cousin," Robert laughed. "She's daddy's girl. But she's no detective, are you, Fanny?"

If I *could* have committed murder, it would have been Robert's right then.

"If you want to be a police officer," Crew said, "go to school. But being a sheriff's daughter doesn't qualify you to consult on my cases."

Double dose of jerk. Fine then, they could be that way. Except he was right, of course, and I was out of line. Except this was my life we were talking about. And I knew enough to be able to read evidence. Guess I had to keep that to myself from now on.

From now on? Like a trail of murders was going to haunt me the rest of my life and make this a common problem or something. Seriously.

"Any idea what Mr. Wilkins was doing on your property?"

And there it was. The elephant in the room question I was hoping he wouldn't ask me. Not like I got a chance to answer it, anyway. Not with the most helpful and thoughtful of best friends in the world who, with a beaming smile and a breathless, wide eyed grasp at Crew's sleeve, stabbed me in the heart and the back with one bright, cheerful statement.

"He said he was Petunia's new owner," Daisy said. "Showed up yesterday with papers and everything." I almost groaned. "Isn't that right, Fee?"

Crew's arched eyebrows told me everything I needed to know. I'd just graduated from pain in his ass to Fiona Fleming, suspect numero uno.

CHAPTER EIGHT

THE HARD, WOODEN SEAT across from the big, wooden table in the small, wooden room hurt my butt. About as much as knowing Daisy, as sweet as she was and as hard as she tried, had not only tossed me to the wolf that Crew had turned into, but had done so with a smile on her face and not a trace of awareness she'd thrown my carcass under the bus.

My suffering cheeks sighed as I shifted and tried to get more comfortable while the blah blah blah of the sheriff's voice washed over me. Because the questions he asked me? Yeah, I'd heard them three times already and stammered through answers all three times, thanks.

I wasn't an idiot. My dad was sheriff for years of this small town and I'd watched enough bad TV to know this kind of pushy, bossy and endlessly wearying tactic was meant to make me break down and cry or confess or something equally stupid. Except I had a secret weapon. See, the five years I'd lived with my lawyer boyfriend, I'd learned how to block him out when he went off on his arrogant spiels about people and things that I didn't give a crap about. Just tuned his ass out completely and thought about things that mattered to me. Even learned to nod and grunt at appropriate moments, so honestly? Being questioned by Crew Turner wasn't that big a deal.

From the increasing redness of his face and the way his shoulders had bunched, he knew he wasn't getting through to me the way he would have liked, though. I wasn't intentionally trying to piss him off. I just didn't know how else to tell him I hadn't drowned that jerk Wilkins in my koi pond regardless of the means, motive and opportunity Crew seemed to think made me his main and only suspect.

"Let's get this straight, for the record." I tuned back in because it sounded for a moment like he might finally be wrapping up. But nope, not really.

Just reiterating what I said in prep for another round of Fiona Fleming, heartless murderer. "You were presented with paperwork that cedes ownership of your B&B by the victim less than twenty-four hours before finding him dead in your back yard—"

"Garden," I muttered for the fourth time because he didn't get the terminology the first three and why, oh why was it men didn't know how to listen?

"—and have no idea how it happened, who killed him or why he died in your pond. Nor do you have an alibi aside from sleeping because no one saw you doing it." He sounded like he believed me. Not. I opened my mouth to protest and his index finger shot into the air, a hissing intake of breath silencing me. "Correction. Aside from your pug, Petunia."

Well, maybe he was listening and was being purposely obtuse. That was worse.

I shrugged and sighed. "I don't know what you want me to say." I couldn't just produce an alibi I didn't have. "I got up this morning, went upstairs, Petunia went out. She barked, I went to check on her. Someone screamed. And boom."

"Boom." Crew sounded less than pleased with my choice of terminology but I was honestly at the end of my own patience by now.

"Splash?" It's not that I wasn't taking this seriously, but I was frankly tired and honestly this was insane.

Crew's left eye twitched.

"I hadn't even seen a lawyer about the papers," I said, sitting forward, trying to diffuse this if I could. "Why would I kill a total stranger who made such a wild claim when I hadn't even confirmed the man wasn't a raving lunatic?"

That made Crew pause at least. You know the worst part of all this? Even being a jerk to me, he was still hot with those deep blue eyes and that wavy black hair and the way he filled out his jeans like there was a lot more to him than a pretty face.

Leave it to me to lust over the very person who thought I was a deranged murderer. But it had been over a month since I slapped Ryan across the face for cheating on me and stormed out of our apartment in New York City. A girl had needs.

Someone slammed a door in the main room of the sheriff's office, just outside Crew's personal space. And it didn't take a rocket scientist—or the booming command that clearly reached my wincing ears—to figure out who had come storming in just then.

Crew's door hit the wall about two seconds later, a small framed photo shaking free from its nail to crash to the floor, glass shattering outward in glittering protest to such treatment. I knew exactly how it felt. I turned, returning circulation in one butt cheek making me flinch as I glanced up and into Dad's furious face.

"Fiona," he said, not looking at me, staring Crew down. "We're leaving. Now."

I stood, old habit. I was my own girl, don't get me wrong. But an early lifetime of doing as my father said wasn't something I forgot. And besides, I was so ready to go.

"I'm not done questioning the suspect." Crew wasn't as loud as Dad, but he was just as firm.

"The *suspect*," Dad snarled, "is lawyering up." He shot me a look that could have set fire to a soggy woodpile. "If she hasn't already."

Whoops. Hadn't I just tried to convince myself I wasn't an idiot? That tuning him out was my best defense? I clearly needed a careful head examination, because I freaking knew better. What was I thinking? That Crew's cuteness meant he wouldn't charge me with murder? That my innocence would protect me? Jeeze, what was wrong with me?

I moved toward Dad in a jerking motion of utter shock, the chair squealing on the wooden floor as I pushed it out of the way with one thigh. Glass crunched under my sneakers, but I was the only one who seemed disturbed by that fact. The two men didn't even glance my way, testosterone flaring between them while the ex-sheriff and his replacement did battle with a pair of steely gazes that actually shook me out of my shock at my own foolishness and instead made me want to smack both of them.

And made my heart stop for the briefest of moments as I realized I hadn't killed Pete Wilkins. But my dad…?

Where was Dad last night?

No, no way. Absolutely not. I rushed to his side, grasped one hand, tugged while my traitor brain gasped at the thought that tracked from start to horrifying finish. He'd been pissed, furious, over the top angry. Rushed out of the house after reading and then crumpling the paperwork. And Mom wouldn't talk about their history, his and Pete's, but it was obvious they had a story that left a lot of bad blood between them. But my father was a police officer for the majority of his life. He would never kill anyone. Not in a way that would get him caught.

Or do so in a way that set up his own daughter for murder.

Fiona Fleming. You stop that right now.

"Dad." He looked down at me at last. "You're right. I want a lawyer." I fixed Crew with my best Fleming stare, no match for the real thing standing next to me but at least we were a united front. "I'm done answering your questions."

Crew grunted but backed off. Looked like it hurt. "Don't leave town, Miss Fleming."

"Where exactly do you think I'm going?" Okay, now I was jacked and you know what? So done thinking this jerk was even remotely attractive. "And can you tell me what single scrap of evidence you have beside the fact the victim was trying to steal my place of business and happened to have the very bad taste to die in my koi pond," Dad snarled at me to shut up but screw that, "and probably poisoned them in the process? You got nada, and we both know it. Because I didn't kill him. And, from what I saw at the scene? Dude slipped in the mud, hit his damned head and drowned his fool self. So you'd better have some excellent evidence the next time you come after me."

So there.

"I'll bear your expert crime scene forensics evaluation in mind," Crew said.

Why did I get the impression he was being sarcastic?

I led the way out, totally done with this entire train wreck that my day had turned into. I caught the sorrowful expression on Toby Miller's face, Dad's former secretary—now Crew's—clearly miserable about the whole thing. But the middle-aged woman who'd been like a second mom when I was small refused to meet my eyes and scrambled for her desk the instant we appeared so I let her have her retreat. Besides, I was a bit distracted when the main door opened and two people stormed in.

The elegantly dressed, dark haired woman wore sunglasses, the young man a scowl, neither looking in Toby's direction but both staring down Dad like he was public enemy number one. The woman seemed familiar, but I couldn't place her but cut myself some slack. It had been a heck of a morning and I hadn't lived here in ten years, after all. Still, something in me said I should know who she was.

Dad stepped aside, pulling me toward him as the pair strode past us and directly into Crew's office, stopping his exit and slamming the door behind them. So no goodbye from the sheriff then?

Toby turned her back on us and I heard a distinctive sniffle from her direction. Dad paused, hurt and worry on his face an instant, a crack forming in the ever present Fleming façade of stone and stern. And then he moved on, stomping past me and out into the late morning sunshine.

Free, if only for the time being, I sighed at the weight that settled over me, the weariness that I still had work to do and questions to answer—and a father's whereabouts to worry about—and followed him outside.

CHAPTER NINE

IT WAS SO BRIGHT outside and the interior of the station so dark I had to blink into the sunlight for a second and, in that moment, ran right into the immovable object that was my dad. He'd come to a halt on the top step and caught me as I squeaked, keeping me upright while I rubbed my nose, sore from the impact with his chest.

"Seriously, warn a girl," I said.

Dad's hand settled around mine and he led me down the steps, longer legs hard to keep up with. I hated that I felt like a little kid running beside her father but that was basically what it amounted to as he dragged me down the street. Dad had stayed fit over the years, not gone to a pot belly like a lot of older men in his generation, so he still felt like the person I was a bit afraid of when I was young. I was imagining the stares and whispers of people we passed, wasn't I?

Oh, Fee.

Half a block from the station I finally jerked my hand out of Dad's and stopped, crossing my arms over my chest and scowling at him because I was in a bad mood already. And being mad at my father for interfering where he wasn't needed, well, that was about right when I finally shook off the daughter complex and regained my independent streak cultivated from a decade outside his influence.

Dad tsked his frustration at me, obviously not happy with my shift in attitude, frowning in return. "What?"

My jaw dropped. "What?" I closed the gap and punched him in the arm. "What was that?"

"That," he growled at me, "was your father rescuing you from being arrested for murder. Because when I heard you were being questioned and hadn't asked for a lawyer," his jaw jumped as he ground the rest out from between clenched teeth, "and realized you'd lost your freaking little mind somewhere between New York and Reading," he exhaled through both nostrils like a bull, "I had to come and save you from yourself."

Toby turned me in, obviously. "I didn't kill anyone," I said. "And I had this under control." Except he was right and I was an idiot but no way—no way—was I telling my dad as much.

"You're just lucky he's too damned arrogant to reach outside his Curtis County jurisdiction and bring the state troopers in." Dad turned and kept walking, forcing me to either run to catch up or lose what he had to say. I chose the former, frustrated and angry I had to it but doing it anyway. "Idiot California cop and his damned West coast attitude."

"So, you don't like Crew, is that what you're trying to say?" It was an old reflex, came from being raised by a hard headed and by the book kind of man like Dad. Jokes seemed to diffuse what backtalk just made worse. But he wasn't buying what I was selling today.

"Just don't say anything else to him from now on," Dad said. "Fee." He stopped again, drew a deep breath and nodded to me, sunlight shining on the silver in his precision cut hair, emotions clearly settling and a bit of concern showing past his granite-like stare. Sure sign Dad was really worried. "We both know you didn't kill Pete Wilkins. But you also know from being my kid just how fast things can go to hell if you say the wrong thing at the wrong time to the wrong person."

"I know." I hugged myself a little, found I was shaking suddenly. "I'm sorry, Dad. I just didn't know what to do. The last thing I expected was to wake up to a dead body this morning."

Dad shrugged. "Welcome home, kid."

He walked on again, slower this time.

"Who were those people?" I glanced behind me the block and a half to the sheriff's office, wondering about the woman in the sunglasses, the angry young man now that I was safe. Damned curiosity seemed to have come back in full force now that I was home. In New York I'd managed to quash my natural need to know things in favor of just getting along. But for some reason this town had woken that instinct all over again. Dad could blame himself, if it came to that. Came by it honestly and all.

"Doesn't matter," Dad said, also typical. "Let's just get you home and get your guests sorted."

Maybe it was a sign of weakness, but when Dad offered his hand again I took it and was grateful for the quiet rest of the walk we shared all the way to my front door.

He didn't linger, not when Daisy came flying out the entry and threw herself into my arms, sobbing. I hugged her, turned her physically around to see my father leaving, already halfway across the street while my old best friend incoherently wept on my shoulder. It took a good minute to get her calmed down to the point I could shove her away and shake her a little.

"Daisy," I said. "It's okay."

"It's *not.*" She wailed her denial. "I'm a *traitor.*"

So she'd finally figured that out, had she? Her weeping guilt was her saving grace. "I didn't kill anyone," I said, leading her inside. "So you didn't do anything wrong." I sighed, letting go of my irritation with her, as always. She'd never stayed in my bad books for long, no matter what happened. Because she never did anything out of malice, just innocent enthusiasm. Wished I had more of that myself. "Crew would have found out about my connection somehow. Best probably to get it out now before he could say I tried to hide it."

She hiccupped around her retreating tears, blinking at me, lower lip trembling as her big eyes shone with every single thing in her truly caring heart. "Really? I thought I sent you to the big house."

Daisy let out one more sob before clutching me in a giant hug. "Are you okay?" She pushed me away this time, looking me up and down in frantic concern. "Did they hurt you? Did he torture you?" Her voice lowered, conspiracy in her tone.

What did she think happened, exactly? "He just asked me some questions. It's okay. Thanks for taking care of things while I was out." I looked down the hall toward the kitchen. "How many guests did we lose?" Olivia's edict or not, I was likely looking at a big loss of revenue this week. Once word got out, guests would be abandoning Petunia's like rats jumping from a burning ship.

"Not a one." Daisy seemed pleased to be able to offer some good news. "In fact, we've had calls to see if we have openings. Everyone loves a good murder." She winced then. "Sorry, too soon?"

I couldn't help the little bark of a laugh that escaped. Just strung too tight to care anyway. "Not soon enough."

"Oh, Fiona dear, there you are." Just what I needed. I pasted a smile over the desire to exhale in irritation as Peggy hurried into the foyer, Cookie dangling from the crook of her arm. The little dog's perky green hair bow bounced on the top of her tiny head. Petunia offered a single woof of greeting which Cookie met with utter silence, as always.

Peggy didn't seem to notice I wasn't really in the mood to talk about what happened because she hugged me one armed, Cookie's little tongue finding my cheek a moment, the strong scent of peppermints and old wool making my nose twitch before Peggy let me go. The thin but strong hand that grasped my arm shook, her face pinched with concern and I relented as she went on.

"I was so worried about you," Peggy said, "and Daisy couldn't tell me much about where you'd gone or what happened."

I patted her hand, feeling myself release of some of the tension I'd clung to the last few hours. "It's going to be okay," I said. "I'm pretty sure it was a tragic accident that killed Mr. Wilkins."

"Oh, how dreadful," Peggy said. "But I don't care about that wretched man, dear." She obviously knew Pete Wilkins, then. I guess I wasn't the only one he'd rubbed the wrong way. No idea why that made me feel better, thinking maybe the whole town hated him. Better than finding the patriarch of Reading drowned in my koi pond. "I was worried about you." She touched my cheek with that same shaking hand, eyes watering. "Iris and I were old friends, Fiona. If she were here she'd be knocking that fool sheriff's head for even considering you were responsible."

From what I remembered about Grandmother Iris, Peggy was right. Made me chuckle this time and that felt good.

"You get yourself sorted," Peggy said. "I know you must have so much to do. But once you find the time, I insist you come for tea. I have some things for you I know your grandmother would have loved for you to keep."

Peggy left on her own accord, waving as she went, and my estimation of her skyrocketed. Nosy, maybe. But she cared, that much was apparent. And I would love to learn more about Grandmother Iris. After this was over.

And after I found out if I still owned Petunia's or not. Or if my father was a murderer.

CHAPTER TEN

WITH THOSE GLUM THOUGHTS chasing me out of the foyer I slumped my way into the kitchen through the swinging door and into the darkly judging domain of the two older ladies who stared at me like they were utterly positive I'd done the deed. Mary and Betty didn't whisper, didn't speak, just watched as I crossed the space to the back door, silently accusing me of murder while my skin crawled.

Faithful to the B&B and old friends of Grandmother Iris or not, I was firing their asses the second I got through this mess.

The sunlight outside felt offensive, grumbling disillusionment and frustration tugging at me about as much as my need to return to the scene of the crime. What was it they said about the guilty hanging around the very place they committed their act of criminal disobedience? And yet, unless I'd sleepwalked my way onto the wrong side of the law, either someone pushed Pete Wilkins or the big idiot slipped and fell and continued with his untimely and poorly placed death to plague me from his grave.

I really had to track down and talk to a lawyer that wasn't Ryan Richards. While I hated that Dad was right, I needed someone to walk me through how to proceed from here, not only with Crew and his ideas about the death of Pete Wilkins, but to find out if in fact the paperwork was authentic. Because despite the truth I'd only been running this place a short time it already felt like home. Even the scent of the flowers that did their best to cheer me up with their summery softness reminded me of childhood. Mind you, I hadn't been allowed to lounge around here or anything. Grandmother Iris expected hard work from her granddaughter if I ever showed up at the B&B. But digging in the dirt to plant new bulbs or learning to make biscuits while she showed me her favorite recipe or even being taught how to dust high shelves without taking down all the nick knacks became summer memories I still found nostalgically appealing.

I never expected her to will Petunia's to me. And though when Mom called to tell me and gave me the exit from New York and Ryan I needed, I never looked back. So there was no way I was giving up this chance at a new start. Not when that new start was still as fresh as the memory of my grandmother's death.

Daisy hovered next to me when I came to a halt at the edge of the police tape, glaring at Robert who threw me a saucy wink before leering at my old best friend. Right, he'd had a crush on her since he was a stringy little psycho who liked to torture girls and push them in puddles. No biases or anything.

"Robert," she gushed, one hand on her bare chest where the third button of her shirt strained to hold things together. "I'm so glad you're still here."

Was she serious? While Peggy had impressed me, Daisy was rapidly falling off my pedestal of people I thought I knew better than to have any kind of compassion or inclination toward my disgusting cousin. My heart plummeted as I stared into the koi pond and realized the scrap of red fabric still hung from the biggest boy's lips. Fat Benny seemed unfazed by the bit of whatever it was he trailed around with him. A clue or not, I really needed to make sure Crew knew about it. No way was I risking him accusing me of hiding evidence.

"Anything you need, Daisy," Robert said in a tone that made me want to throw up all over his cowboy boots. Seriously, where did he think he was wearing jeans and boots instead of the rest of his standard uniform? The Wild West? And the tilt to his hat, that was an attempt at cowboy confidence that just made him look pathetic. God, that mustache.

Gross.

Never mind Crew set the precedent. It looked good on him. On Robert? Shudder.

Daisy glanced at me before leaning closer to my deputy cousin. "I hear the sheriff thinks it was an accident."

Robert puffed up, chest out, just managing to hide the beginnings of his beer bulge, preening like the idiot peacock he was and Daisy lapped it up. Any second now she'd be purring. And I'd be contaminating the crime scene with the contents of my stomach. A huge feat considering I hadn't had anything to eat since Mom's chocolate cake last night.

Hard not to roll my eyes. At least she was a distraction. He completely ignored me while I sidled sideways toward the pond, his attention totally focused on Daisy. There had to be proof here this was an accident. I could see it all, really. How Pete poked around after dark, slipped on the fresh mud I'd turned at the edge of the pond for the new flowers I planted, hit his head on the rock then rolled, unconscious, into the water. Simple, right? And the clear answer. Although why he was here remained a mystery. Surely he could have waited two more days. Especially if his ownership of this place was authentic. Whatever brought him here, that was part of the mystery I couldn't shake or let go.

Petunia chuffed softly, but not at my feet as usual. I turned toward her, frowning then. Wait, I'd totally forgotten. She'd woken me up in the middle of the night, hadn't she? Barked at something. Did she wake up when Pete died? Was she trying to warn me he was there or even alert me he had fallen? The idea I'd gone back to sleep while the man drowned finally triggered my compassion, paperwork or no paperwork. No one deserved to die alone like that.

But there was still that odd mark in the ground a few feet from where it looked like he slipped. A round indentation with a strange impression on the bottom about an inch deep, perfect ridges left behind. What made that particular marking? Maybe a tourist dropped something and I didn't notice and this had nothing at all to do with the murder. Just like the agonizingly tempting piece of red cloth that Fat Benny trailed from the corner of his fishy lips as he lazily slid by.

Something pattered against my leg and I finally turned, found Petunia digging about five feet away. Far enough from the crime scene I wasn't worried Crew would be pissed, but seriously. Not a good idea. I huffed an irritated breath and went to her, to stop her. And stared down as she sat abruptly, smiling up at me in her pug way with her tongue hanging out, corkscrew tail wiggling. But I wasn't looking at her any longer. Far more interesting was the corner of what looked like a small, metal box she'd uncovered in the middle of the next flower bed.

The instant my brain told me I should turn this find in to the authorities my mind rejected the idea so abruptly I gasped.

"Something wrong, Fanny?" I had caught Robert's attention, and he didn't seem happy about it, though the smile on Daisy's face was far more strained than I expected for someone who seemed content to flirt with the vile creature. His body swayed as if about to take a step closer when I smiled and shook my head, forgetting for once how much I hated that nickname, one foot casually kicking at some dirt, not sure if I covered the box's peeking edge or not.

"Just wondering how long this is going to clutter up my garden." Rather rude, but he expected nothing less and it had the desired effect. Robert smirked at me, shrugged, settled back into his stay put stance.

"It'll take as long as it takes." He winked at Daisy once more.

Petunia turned and I knew immediately she planned to start digging again. Knowing the desperation in my voice had to be apparent, I did my best to smile through it. "Daisy," I bent and grabbed the pug around her substantial chest, all twenty-five pounds of her dead weight sliding through my arms. "Can you please take Petunia inside?"

"Of course!" She dodged for the dog, hefting her much more kindly than I had, cradling her almost like a toddler with an arm around her chest and one hand supporting her rear. The pug grunted at me, front paws flinging dirt as she swung them at me before swiping Daisy's cheek with her tongue. "Let's get you a snack and a drink, young lady. Robert." She nodded to him before retreating. I made sure he was watching her go before risking a glance down and scooping a bit more dirt with the heel of my sneaker to be sure the corner of the mystery box was hidden before stepping firmly on the spot to finish the job. And looked up just in time as Robert returned his attention from Daisy's retreating sway of a walk to me.

"Nice to see you're a valuable member of the team," I said as I strode past. "Great job guarding the fish, Booby."

The snarl he fired after me was so worth it. Because, of course I had a childhood tit-for-tat to throw at him. And, hopefully, enough distraction he wouldn't notice the footprint I'd left in the flowerbed. Like that useless excuse would notice a clue if it stuck to him like a leech. I knew, as I crossed to the house, I really should have just turned in the box. Was fairly confident it had nothing to do with the murder, so what hurt would it do? But I did love a good mystery. Knowing Crew he'd hang onto it for ages and I'd never get it back. Convinced myself then and there the fact it was buried in the garden didn't mean it had anything to do with Pete Wilkins or his death. If anything, it was a private matter between me and Grandmother Iris. Consoled my guilt with the assurance if there did turn out to be evidence proving murder, I'd naturally give it to Crew.

After I had a chance to dig up that box and find out what the old lady thought was so important she had to hide it underground.

CHAPTER ELEVEN

THE KITCHEN'S AIR OF gloom had lifted when I entered the house, Mary and Betty both absent for once. And the minute I entered Daisy rushed to me, Petunia gobbling at the chunks of kibble and cheese in her giant bowl. I winced, knowing I'd suffer the lactose consequences later, but didn't comment, not when my old bestie flung her arms around my neck and hugged me.

"I hope that at least made up for it a bit," she said, shuddering as she pulled back. "He's a creep, but you seemed to want to have a look around." Wait, what? Daisy bit her lower lip, as hang dog as I'd ever seen her. A honey blonde curl escaped from the pretty pink band she used to hold her hair back today, matching her bright blouse perfectly. "Did I do okay?"

I couldn't help the grin that broke over my face and, on impulse, hugged her back. She squeaked in surprise but embraced me with gusto as I giggled in her ear.

"I thought you'd lost your good taste and your mind there for a minute," I said. "Robert, of all people."

She snorted, adorably of course. "Can I just say *ew*? Like, *ew* to the *ewiest*." We laughed together for a moment before she sobered. "I feel so bad, Fee." Daisy sank to a stool, one that Betty usually occupied, the older woman's large backside barely supported though my best friend's tiny one fit it perfectly. "I know I'm a flake a lot of the time and that people think I'm stupid." I chewed on the inside of my cheek in guilt because yeah, I was one of them. "I don't always think before I talk and there are things I don't understand sometimes." She seemed close to tears while the utter genuineness of her made me want to cry with her for being so hard on her. Sure, she'd dumped more than she should have to Crew, but so what? He was going to find out anyway. I was a horrible, horrible person for thinking badly of her. "But I'm really sorry and I promise I'll try harder."

"Daisy, it's honestly okay." I sank against the counter, staring down at Petunia who waddled to my side, squatting on her butt with her back legs sticking straight forward, utterly pleased with her snack and likely looking for more to eat. "I'm so glad you're here." My friend lost her agonized hurt look and perked. "And you did awesome with Robert. I just hope that doesn't come back to bite you later."

She tossed her blonde curls, long lashes closing over one gray eye. "I have it handled," she said. And laughed.

Way smarter than I ever thought she was.

Daisy kicked butt the rest of the day, handling guests like an utter pro—they always loved her regardless of her quirks and occasional mess-ups—not a disaster to be had. I avoided the baleful glares of the Jones sisters lurking as they always did in the background and instead focused on finishing all the big and small tasks that needed to be done every day to keep Petunia's running and legal. Like cleaning, paperwork, more cleaning, more paperwork. By the time the sun was setting and Mary and Betty long gone, I wearily descended to the foyer to find Daisy closing the appointment app on the sideboard computer with a happy sigh, the phone settling in the cradle from a finished call.

"All booked up for the next two months," she said, bright and cheerful, enough to make me smile. "We only have one night open the end of September and thanks to the big push the mayor is making for the ski lodge for the fall, it looks like shoulder season won't be much quieter."

I'd take that as good news regardless of whether I was still Petunia's owner or not. Filling up before or after the main season was over meant bigger revenue. Someone else's revenue? Something to be tackled in the morning. For now, I was grateful for a tired body and mind and the chance, very shortly, to fall into bed and forget this day ever happened.

I sent Daisy home with another hug and my thanks, checking in on the garden as the sun set behind the mountains. A young female deputy nodded to me, her blonde ponytail the only indication of her sex, body tucked into a more official uniform and jacket. I waved and retreated, hesitating before digging out a snack from the fridge and bringing it to her.

"Thank you." She seemed startled by the sandwich and canned soft drink. Didn't hurt to ingratiate myself with at least one person on the sheriff's payroll. A quick glance at the flower bed told me no one had uncovered the box Petunia dug up and I sloppily hid, the impression of my sneaker a red flag banner no one else apparently saw as evidence. It was too dark to see the koi, so I didn't comment about Fat Benny to the deputy, leaving well enough alone for now. If the fish decided to finally swallow the scrap, so be it.

I left her munching on chicken salad and ducked downstairs to my apartment for a quick collapse on the sofa with my feet up on the old coffee table. Petunia grunted her way up next to me, throwing her full weight against me as she collapsed and settled her wide, silly head on my lap. Those giant brown eyes stared up at me, black ears perked while she grumbled a few choice complaints until I rubbed at her cheeks and made her groan.

"What a day, pug." Now that I'd come to a sudden halt, everything crashed down on me again. The overwhelming truth of what had happened paralyzed me and left me breathless. A man died in my back yard after claiming he owned my business. A business that might now belong to his heir while the sheriff was investigating me for murder. Evidence more than likely remained in my yard, at the very least in the jaws of the koi and most probably—if I was willing to admit it—in the metal box buried in the flower bed.

And my dad might have killed Pete Wilkins.

I sat abruptly upright, Petunia muttering her displeasure at this state of not resting affairs. I had to talk to Pete's family, find out about the deed. If in fact Grandmother Iris did sign over Petunia's, why? And could they be talked into some kind of arrangement?

It was too soon after his death to just go barging over there, wasn't it?

Maybe. But a lawyer, yes. First priority. I sank back into the cushions of the old sofa, intending to get up, check the grounds one last time, that my guests were secure and the house locked up. While Petunia's head settled once more in my lap and her eyes closed.

I blamed the dog for me waking in an uncomfortably awkward position, half sideways on the paisley fabric with a drool trail wetting the faded velvet nap. Movement in the kitchen over my head told me it was morning, as much as the light beaming in the windows, washing across my face and adding to my confusion.

Petunia abandoned me for upstairs, fine by me. A shower and my own brewed coffee later—stronger than any guest would be willing to drink but just the ticket this morning—and I was feeling up to facing the day. Betty didn't even acknowledge me as I entered the kitchen, but Mary made sure, as she hustled through the swinging door with the first plates of morning dirty dishes in her hands, I saw her frown of unhappiness.

"Just say it." I was done with her attitude, with both of them. "Go on, say it. How Grandmother Iris did such a good job and I'm messing everything up and how could I allow someone to try to take Petunia's like that and how could I have murdered a man in our own yard?" I huffed through that tirade as Mary gaped at me. Even Betty spun in slow motion to stare, her bushy gray eyebrows climbing so high the lines in her forehead met each other in overlapping pink flesh. "Say it so we can just get on with things and have done with it."

Mary's lips moved but nothing came out. And that, I have to say, was the most satisfying sound I'd ever heard.

Instead of waiting for her to gather her wits, I strode past her and into the garden, needing a moment to catch my breath before I came face to face with a guest. The mood I was in this morning? They'd get both barrels even if they asked for extra toilet paper. And let me tell you, being a B&B newbie owner? There was nothing more frustrating than guests and excess toilet paper.

Some things *were* worth murdering over.

CHAPTER TWELVE

THE MOMENT OF PEACE I needed, however, vanished in a puff of irritated breath at the sight of Crew and the female deputy—Robert standing around doing nothing while his boss and coworker wound up tape—cleared the crime scene. That should have made me happy, right?

Grumble at least tell me what happened mumble.

Crew's scowl had to match mine as I stomped to a halt at his side and glared up at him. "Well?"

He grunted, gritted his teeth. "The coroner," he said like it hurt him to speak, "has ruled Pete's death an accident."

"I see." Vindication, oh yeah.

"But." So he wasn't letting this go, was he? "There's an odd bruise on the victim's leg that isn't accounted for and I still have to explain a few more things before I'm satisfied with that ruling."

Actually, I wasn't 100% sold on the whole accident thing myself, oddly, so I didn't argue despite knowing it meant I wasn't in the clear yet. Stubborn knew stubborn, after all. That glint of a dog with a bone he couldn't let go of wasn't lost on me because I was gnawing my own, wasn't I?

"That said," Crew went on, "I'm willing to release the scene at this point."

I choked on spewing about the box. But he noticed, because I was obvious and an idiot.

"Was there something you wanted to disclose, Miss Fleming?" He had to use that snarky tone that made me want to smack him, didn't he? "Something you want to confess?"

"Only," I sniped back, thankful one of the koi swam by right then and reminded me I had more than one bit of possible evidence to lure him with, "that your deputies need glasses. Or training." I pointed at Fat Benny. Thankfully, the idiot fish still hadn't managed to swallow his little red trailer. "While I'm not positive it's part of the crime, you might want to collect actual evidence in an actual crime scene before the local fauna decides it's dinner."

If I thought Crew looked irritated before? Well, that was an interesting vein he had in his forehead, the kind that bulged and pulsed in a lightning bolt shape under the skin in a way that could lead to an aneurism if he wasn't careful.

"Deputy Carlisle," Crew snarled. "Get that fish."

I stepped out of the way, unable to restrain my grin of delight at the sight of Robert sloshing around in my pond trying to catch Fat Benny. For a chubby koi of excessive size, he could move when he wanted to. Finally, her face twisted into a disgusted grimace, his fellow deputy lunged while Robert pounced and the pair came up with the scrap of red.

Definitely fabric, some kind of ribbon. It disappeared into a clear plastic sleeve before I could get a closer look. The glare on Crew's face was worth it, though I caught him glancing around the garden then and cursed myself for saying anything. Because it would be just like him to slap up the damned police tape again and do a more thorough search of the entire garden. No way would he miss finding the box at that point.

I stumbled sideways as he took a half step in the wrong direction, right toward the place Petunia had been digging. I smiled up at him, did my best perky while the corner of the box bit into the bottom of my thin sneaker just under the surface of the dirt.

"In case you forgot," I said, "you were just leaving."

He didn't comment, hands on hips, looking around the yard while my heart beat grew louder and stronger in my chest. He knew, he'd seen the corner sticking out. Or he suspected I was hiding something. At the very least I was giving myself away right now. Why I felt so protective of the box I had no idea, only that he would be digging it up and taking it away over my dead body.

And there had been enough death in this yard for my liking, thanks.

Crew looked down at me, narrowed eyes unreadable. "If you find anything else, Miss Fleming," he said.

And then I understood. He wasn't leaving the scene because he wanted to. If Crew Turner had his way, he'd dig up the entire garden just to see what was here. He was being pressured. By my dad? No, by someone far scarier than John Fleming.

"Say hello to Olivia for me when you see her," I said with just enough snark I triggered his vein and eye twitch at exactly the same time. I really shouldn't have baited him, nor cackled inside like a maniac at his reaction. I should have been doing my best to work with him and help him solve the case. Maybe. Didn't keep me from stepping aside and gesturing for the door to the kitchen.

"I'm sure you'll keep me posted," I said. And waited.

So satisfying to see him show himself out. Why, oh why then did that very nicely shaped posterior give me such delight to watch? Not just because he was leaving. I was honest enough with myself to admit it.

Even after everything, damn that man was delicious.

The instant I shifted my weight to my left foot I winced and remembered. Looked down at the little corner of the box as I moved my sneaker out of the way. I had to dig this thing up and now. Before Crew found a way around the mayor's bullying and came back to finish the job of ruining my life.

Petunia's woof warned me, raised my head and though the smiling and waving Peggy over the fence was about the least threatening thing that had happened to me in the last two days, I still hesitated. The sweet old lady would have a million questions about the box, I imagined, and the part of me that wanted to protect it didn't even want an old friend of Grandmother Iris's to lay eyes on it before I knew what was inside.

Dad may have talked me out of becoming an actual detective, but he couldn't take the curiosity I was born with away.

I waved back, kicking more dirt in a show of being irritated with the cops and the mess they left behind before heading for the house, Petunia at my heels. I'd come out here tonight and dig it up when no one was looking. Hide it in the wheelbarrow with weed cuttings. Perfect.

And very satisfying, considering.

A feeling that fizzled out when I entered the kitchen to Daisy's smile. Not that I wasn't happy to see her—and on time for once—but the small, wrapped box with the beautiful red bow in her hands made me stop and stare. And wince.

"Can you please make sure Lucy gets this for me?" Mom's birthday. I'd totally forgotten. Damn it. I took the present from Daisy as she blushed faintly.

"I know she hates gifts, but I wanted her to have something." Daisy tinkled a giggle, her multiple silver bangles jingling in tune with her laugh, the pretty blue dress she wore today making her look right out of the 50's.

"Thanks, Daisy," I said. "I'll take it tonight."

And, promptly forgot. Naturally.

CHAPTER THIRTEEN

IT WASN'T UNTIL ALMOST 4:30 I noticed the beautifully wrapped box sitting next to the phone on the sideboard desk in the foyer that I remembered again. The smiling couple who climbed the stairs with their luggage thumping behind them forgotten, I lunged for the small box, heard the rattle and felt my heart shrivel.

Mom. Groan.

With Petunia in tow, balancing my oversized purse, my phone, car keys and the present from Daisy—while she leaned out the front door and waved and beamed a smile with a, "Have fun!" that made me cringe—I lurched into the driver's seat of my car and waited for the chubby pug to heave herself over to her own side before slamming the door.

Yes, my hands were full. Yes, I had a purse. Yes, it was too crammed with crap I meant to clean out for anything else to fit. I shoved the worn brown leather—my favorite bag ever for its softness and durability when it came to handling my life—down beside the passenger seat of my little hatchback, buckling Petunia's body harness into the seatbelt and making sure her airbag was off before slamming the car into gear and chugging away downtown.

I could have walked, but dinner was at 6:00 which really meant 5:30 in Lucy Fleming time. Considering my mother was making her own birthday meal, I just couldn't be late. And I'd forgotten all about the flowers Dad asked me like a week ago to pick up for her for tonight because he didn't want a delivery car showing up at the house or something silly like that. And, of course, I'd completely dropped the ball leading me to race as fast as I could in the 20mph speed zones and with the complaining old engine of my little compact huffing at me because I hadn't driven her much since we got to Reading.

"Please," I whispered into the windshield. "Just let me get through tonight."

Don't get me wrong. I loved my parents. And Mom was a fantastic cook. But Dad wasn't the most demonstrative of people and I ended up trying to make up for that, creating an awkward and disjointed conversation over food that should have been served in an upscale restaurant while Dad picked at it like it was going to bite him. While visibly contemplating getting a burger later.

Families. So messy.

I pulled into a vacant spot just outside the main door of Jacob's Flowers with a whispered thank you to the parking genies for granting me their favors. Petunia's leash immediately wrapped around my ankles and I spent about thirty seconds turning in circles one direction while she did the same in the other, winding us tighter together. I glared down at her, feeling ridiculous and out of breath and utterly frustrated.

And laughed at the flustered look on her pug face.

"Okay," I said. "Hold still." A quick unhooking and unwinding and we were on our way inside the flower shop, my mood greatly elevated. Who knew having a dog around could be anything but irritating? Dad never let me have a pet when I was a kid, didn't want the responsibility. And I'd kept that attitude even in New York. My memories of the other Petunias were vague and often gross—being licked in the face, snorted on, sat on, farted at—and hadn't endeared me to the idea of taking on Madam Petunia Her Highness the Fourth. But the more time I spent with her, the more she grew on me. Imagine that.

The glass door tinkled a welcome, bells hanging from the hinges signaling my entry. I inhaled a moment, taking in the mixed scents of the lush foliage hanging from the ceiling, the expanse of cases humming behind the counter while Petunia snuffled curiously at the lower displays with a rather royal air.

"Can I help you?" I'd never seen her before, the girl behind the counter. Well, girl was being rude. She was about my age, I guessed, close to thirty, but considering I still thought of myself as eighteen I figured the term was fair game. I crossed to the tidy glass counter where she waited, her long, dark hair caught in a low pony, skin that delightful color between milk chocolate and mocha. Big, brown eyes smiled at me, her Indian heritage obvious in her appearance and the faint accent she spoke in.

"I'm picking up an order for John Fleming." At least Dad wouldn't have forgotten to place it. I don't think my father ever forgot anything in his entire life. "Red roses?" Of course, red roses. So original. He could have just picked up his flowers himself, couldn't he? I privately grumbled in my head, though I knew what he'd say if I called him on it.

"They're from both of us," he'd mumble in his growly voice. "Your mother would like that."

Not a sentimental bone in that man's body. Seriously. And Mom a romance novel addict who loved everything to do with *l'amore*. Opposites attract, indeed. I really shouldn't have been whining about it anyway. Sure, I was dealing with a murder and the possible loss of Petunia's and an overflow of guests, but this was my mom.

Bad daughter.

The woman disappeared the moment I mentioned Dad and left me to stare down at Petunia who panted at the reflection of herself in the glass counter, propped up in her usual seated pose as if admiring what she saw. I needed to take her casual admiration to heart and apply some of it to myself. I couldn't remember the last time I put on mascara or even really did my hair. Daisy's polished beauty she managed to maintain no matter what had as yet to rub off on me in any kind of meaningful way. And if

I was going to be honest, I hadn't really taken much time to see to my appearance since I walked out on Ryan. Nope, not thinking about that jerk right now, forget it. Except his favorite thing to do when he screwed up—often and horribly and I always took him back because I was an idiot—was to slather the apartment in flowers.

The young woman returned, a thankful distraction. I was starting to get the creeps in here just thinking about him.

"Here you are. I hope the design is all right." So soft spoken. Her shy smile triggered an auto response and I smiled back. The bouquet was gorgeous, a dozen lovely, fat buds surrounded by green and a cluster of other flowers in complimentary pink and yellow snuggled inside a sleeve of plastic.

"Perfect." I rifled into my bag for my wallet, but she shook her head.

"They're already paid for," she said. "Sheriff Fleming—I mean, Mr. Fleming," she flushed, dark cheeks deep pink, "called in his credit card. Funny, he wouldn't let us deliver?"

I shrugged. "That's my dad." My wallet dropped back into the quagmire of disaster that was my purse and I tossed the flap over to hide the mess. "Is Mr.

Jacob retired then?" I had memories of the previous owner from all the times Dad dragged me in here to take possession of flowers he bought for Mom. As the young woman answered, I made a parallel between Ryan and my father and had a horrible thought—despite swearing I never would, had I been dating my dad?

"My husband and I took over the business three years ago," she said, offering her hand in a hesitant gesture that made me wonder if she wasn't quite comfortable with putting herself out there. "Terri Jacob."

I shook firmly and kindly. "Fiona Fleming."

"Ah!" Terri's face altered from nervous to brightly happy. "Simon's told me about you. You went to school together."

We did, though I barely remembered him aside from the fact he was quiet and played the cello.

"How is Mr. Jacob?" I recalled always being fascinated with him as a girl. Reading was a fairly solid white town and his skin tone caught and held my attention every time. So beautiful and rich looking, exotic in a sea of Caucasian boredom. It wasn't until I moved to New York and discovered diversity I realized just how sheltered I'd been my entire life. So lovely now to realize the faces I passed on the street lately here were nicely mixed thanks to tourism and immigration.

Terri's face fell and she shook her head. "So sad," she said. "He's passed. He had dementia. We tried for over a year to take care of him, but we had to finally find somewhere to care for him." That was a whole lot of guilt right there. And honestly, I guess if it was me I'd feel the same way. Especially if Mom was gone and Dad was on his own. To put him in a hospital or a nursing home? Yikes. "You took over Petunia's when Mrs. Iris passed?"

I nodded and winced. "I guess I should ask how bad it is. Are people talking about the… you know?" She was a fellow business owner, so I had no qualms asking.

Her big eyes widened further. "The murder?" She whispered it like no one knew.

"The very thing." I looked down into Mom's roses through the plastic covering them. "Couldn't have happened to a nicer guy." Sarcasm, my dear friend.

Terri snorted like she agreed with me and I perked.

"Good riddance to that man, I say," she said. Then covered her mouth with both hands in horror. "I'm a terrible person."

"Well, he wasn't much better," I said, curiosity piqued. "I take it you had a run in?"

She hugged herself then, nodded quickly. I had the distinct feeling then Terri Jacob didn't get to talk to many people outside of her job because she seemed pretty eager to chat with me. "We almost lost the flower shop to that horrible man," she said. "He showed up here one morning, just after Ranjeet—Mr. Jacob—entered the nursing home, with paperwork that said he'd signed over our property to Mr. Wilkins." She shook her head while my heart stopped beating and I stood frozen, staring like she'd just hit me.

He *what*?

Terri went on as if my utter surprise encouraged her. "It's true, I swear it."

"Terri?" I started at the interruption, inhaling sharply when the tall, slim man who had entered the back without my noticing approached the counter with a scowl and concern in his dark eyes. Simon Jacob nodded to me once in acknowledgement before speaking again. "We don't talk about our private business in public."

She gulped but smiled at her husband, patting his arm like he was a dear pet she adored. "Simon, you remember Fiona?"

I stuck out my hand which he reluctantly shook, not meeting my eyes. Just as I remembered him from school. "Terri was telling me about your encounter with Pete Wilkins."

"It doesn't matter anymore," Simon muttered. "The man's dead."

Well, that was an interesting thing to say. I opened my mouth to ask about the deed issue only to have Terri finish without prompting.

"The matter is all taken care of," she said, proudly beaming at Simon who just looked unhappy. "Simon talked to Mr. Wilkins and straightened it out. A complete misunderstanding."

Either my old classmate was a miracle worker and I needed his help or something wasn't right about this. It was possible the papers were forged and Simon managed to confront Wilkins about it. But from the uneasy way he shuffled his feet and refused to meet my eyes, it was far more likely Simon Jacob wasn't telling his wife everything.

And that, if my backyard body was murdered, I just found another suspect.

CHAPTER FOURTEEN

THE FRONT DOOR BELLS jingled, distracting me from grilling Simon about what happened. I half turned before my gut lurched and everything about my day turned to ash and gray. I'd done my best to avoid the stunning ice blonde in the perfect yellow suit who simpered on her clicky clacking high heels into the flower shop with her giant designer glasses perched on the end of her pointed nose and so far I'd succeeded. Just the odd chance glance across a crowded street or over the windshield of her little red convertible. But this was the first time since I moved home I actually came face to face with the one person in Reading I would gladly have trade places with Pete Wilkins.

If the way she pulled down her glasses with overly pointed and painted manicure nails and glared at me was any indication, she was about as happy to see me as I was her. Vivian French—her name as pretentious as the rest of her—smiled her reptile greeting with dead blue eyes and slowed her approach to a challenging strut, cute little bag bouncing over her forearm while she looked me up and down.

I hadn't really worried about my looks despite my envy of Daisy's beauty. It's never been something I took into much consideration. I knew I had nice hair, thick and wavy and that deep red my friends in New York always accused me came from a bottle despite being natural. And my green eyes had that clarity I knew a lot of people wore contacts for. I'd always had clear skin, even as a teen, a great figure despite a terrible diet and irregular exercise and the kind of height that allowed me to feel unintimidated by the majority of men thanks to my dad. But there was something about the way my old rival, the former high school cheer squad leader/homecoming queen/overall pain in my younger ass looked at me—judged me—that made me forget former possible murder victims and consider new ones.

"Why, Fanny Fleming." Oh my God, if one more person called me Fanny I was honestly going to lose my mind. I knew Vivian used it on purpose, just like Robert did. They'd been friends in high school, after all, or at least co-conspirators against my happiness. Part of the reason I couldn't wait to cut and run ten years ago. "My word and stars. I heard you were home. And under investigation for murder, no less." She was loving this, I could tell, how she cocked her hip to one side, slim body posing inside her expensive suit. Personally I thought that shade of yellow made her look sallow and gave her bleached hair a straw like appearance.

"Vivs," I said, just as sweet, the tightening around her eyes barely reaching the line between them, a sure sign of work done. I'd seen enough Botox injections in my friends to know it when it glared me in the face. "Nice suit."

Funny how easy it was to fall back into old ways of being and despising. Honestly, I was a grown up wasn't I? And yet, nope, not at all. I was eighteen again and couldn't stand the sight of the precious bitch who pursed her pink lips at me.

"I've been meaning to stop in," she said. "To Petunia's." The pug made a soft grumbling sound like she'd rather not. Vivian glanced down with a faint frown of disgust before her smile returned, shining white teeth a mouthful of Chicklets no one would ever believe were real.

"Still living in Reading, are you?" I leaned one elbow on the counter, too wrapped up in this encounter to care at the moment Simon had vanished, though Terri continued to watch, eyes massive, mouth hanging slightly open as if unsure exactly what was going on. Poor thing. She clearly didn't yet get the subtleties of Vivian French's layers of gross.

Another hit, Fee 2, Vivs whatever, who cared. "I've taken over Daddy's business," she said, all airs and pomposity. "French's Handmade Bakery is now in four states."

Well la de da. I hated the snake of jealousy that bit deep inside me. No way she was allowed to be more successful than me. Of course, she had Daddy's business and a head start, so there.

"I'm surprised to hear you came back from New York." Fishing, was she? "That handsome boyfriend of yours, the lawyer. What's his name?"

How the hell did she know about Ryan? "It's over," I growled.

Fake concern met sisterly caring as she touched my arm with the barest caress meant to mean nothing while her sharp blue eyes crinkled as much as they could in her delight. The faintest rims of contact lenses told me the false intensity of the color was due to tinting. Naturally. "Oh, how sad for you. And to lose Iris that way." She shook her head, blonde locks swinging around her shoulders, tsking. "Then this hideous murder and you being questioned and everything." She knew far more than she should and her next statement told me why. "I'm sure Crew will clean up your mess before you know it."

The way she said his name told me everything. They were either dating or had dated or had some kind of emotional connection that burned my socks so badly at the idea I'd even considered that creep attractive I wanted to scrape my tongue from the bitter taste that dried out my mouth.

I could have been the bigger person and just let it go. Yup, I sure could have, because that would be mature and turning the other cheek and stuff like that. Instead, I leaned closer to her, squinting a little, before grinning.

"Do you remember the day I punched you in sixth grade and broke your nose?" I had, too. She'd been picking on Daisy. It was the first time we crossed swords, really. She'd ignored me as unimportant and unworthy until that afternoon on the playground when I'd had enough of her taunting the kind girl who didn't get she was being played and wound up with a solid blow to the bridge of Vivian's pointed proboscis.

She flinched at the memory, one hand rising as if in defense.

"Can still see the break," I winked. And left, Petunia chuffing beside me, while Vivian's horrified examination of her nose in the glass gave me great pleasure.

Fee—3. Vivian nada, zero, go choke yourself.

CHAPTER FIFTEEN

I DABBED AT THE corner of my mouth with the soft, white napkin and sighed in happiness. Mom had outdone herself and from the beaming way she looked at my empty plate, I'd given her the best birthday present ever.

"I hope you saved room for dessert." She hustled to her feet, the padded bottoms of the dining room chair silent on the hardwood floor as she stood across from me, rushing around Dad to take my plate. I knew better than to try to help, smiling up at her before scowling a bit at my father as Mom divested him of his, too. Usually he did a good job of at least trying to compliment Mom on her amazing cooking despite his lack of enthusiasm for her culinary explorations. Instead, tonight of all nights, he stared at his glass of beer and grunted when she swooped in and took the fine white china plate from in front of him before sweeping off toward the kitchen. Naturally, drooling and hoping for scraps, Petunia followed her, claws clicking on the floor.

I let her go, focused on Dad. I could just reach him at the head of the table with the toe of my shoe, catching his shin with a satisfying blow that raised his head and earned me a frown.

"That was delicious, Mom," I called out, tilting my head and glaring at him. "The best pork loin I've ever tasted." I wasn't lying to make her feel better, either. Whatever she'd marinated the meat in gave it a tangy sweetness mixed with spice that melted in the mouth and paired perfectly with the mushroom sauce she'd ladled generously over the garlic mashed potatoes. And forget about the glaze she'd used on the carrots. I'd take a shower in it.

Dad winced and looked away when Mom peeked her head around the corner, pug still stalking her, carefully styled hair caught at the base of her neck to keep it out of the way of her cooking. "Thank you, sweetie," she said. "I'm trying a new rub. Did you really like it?" My mother was an amazing woman and had a core of steel hidden carefully behind charm and her own brand of sophistication. She'd managed Dad all these years without a complaint or a scrap of concern, even when he handled really horrible cases and wasn't fit to live with. But when it came to cooking, she was her own worst enemy and had insecurities just like the rest of us.

You know what? Mom deserved to trust her talent and I did everything I could to support her cooking habit. Including eating everything she made with gusto. And if a little bit of excessive praise kept my tummy happy… I'd forgotten just how good she was at this.

"Mom, you'd put a chef at the finest overpriced New York joint to shame." Another kick for Dad who shot me a scowl before piping up himself.

"Fantastic, Lu," he said, voice loud enough I knew she heard. "What Fee said."

He did *not* just cop out like that. "You can't possibly top that with dessert," I said, tossing my napkin at him and jutting my lower jaw so he knew how much trouble he was in dropping the ball like this. On Mom's birthday.

Dad sighed then, sipped his beer. "I couldn't dream of ruining the symphony of perfection that's still lingering in my mouth with mere *sugar*," he said. And stuck his tongue out at me.

Well, that was at least an effort.

Mom appeared at the door, breathless. "You two have no idea," she squealed before disappearing again.

I leaned toward Dad who had returned to staring into his beer. "Crew says the coroner thinks Pete's death is an accident." I hissed that at him, caught his annoyed attention. Did he look suddenly guilty? Or relieved? No way of knowing which, not with my most stoic of Dads glaring me down. "But what if he was pushed?"

"By who, Fee?" Dad's low tone matched mine. Neither of us wanted Mom in on this. She'd be so disappointed, cop talk on her birthday. "You?"

I snarled at him. "Cute," I said, almost blurting a repeat of his question—refusing to believe while struggling not to—before sharing what I'd learned. "But I do know the whole signing over of Petunia's isn't the first time he tried such a scheme."

Dad leaned in himself then, focused for real now. I'd finally caught his attention. "You stay out of this, Fee," he said in that growling commanding voice of his that stopped working on me when I was twelve and knew he'd never follow through with any punishment he set. That was Mom's job, delivered in a disappointed voice but with a will of iron might I could never win against. Who knew? "I mean it."

Which meant Dad was well aware there were other victims like me. "I can't just drop this, Dad," I said. "The man died at my place. While claiming it wasn't my place anymore. And he's tried the same thing with others." Frustration made my hands clench into fists on either side of my now empty place mat. "I need answers."

"It's got nothing to do with you," Dad said, "and I'm taking care of Petunia's. So just mind your own business."

Mom reappeared with an enthusiastic, "Ta-da!" and a giant cheesecake on a tray, a ring of sliced strawberries drizzled in vanilla sauce making a crown of crimson and white around the edge. Petunia settled right beside Mom, staring up at her with the whites of her brown eyes showing, eagerly anticipating her own slice. Mom's return silenced my conversation with Dad. We both ate the delicious and decadent treat like it was a race, me glaring at him over my berries, him staring right back until, as usual, he beat me, cramming the last massive bite down before springing to his feet and saluting Mom with his still dirty fork. Petunia chuffed an impatient yip at him for not even saving her a crumb while he spoke.

"Delicious," he said around his mouthful. At least, that's what I think he said. Before spinning and leaving the room.

The coward. I barely tasted my cheesecake to that point, and turned to find Mom sadly watching Dad go. Instantly felt terrible for ruining my mother's birthday and slowed the hell down. Said yes to a second piece which I picked at while Mom played with her own with a low, sad sigh.

"Dinner was awesome," I said, reaching out to squeeze her hand. Petunia muttered her dissatisfaction with being ignored, forgiving Mom instantly as she bent and offered the pug a little lick of cheesecake off her finger before sitting up again.

I knew that look on Mom's face. She smiled bravely at me, setting down her fork with a tiny tinkle of silver on china. "I should know better than to think you two could have a civil dinner with everything that's going on." She patted my hand, her green eyes my green eyes. "And I shouldn't have tried."

"Mom." I tugged at her fingers when she attempted to rise and leave. "Wait, please." The flowers were already in a vase in the kitchen, suitably adored and lovingly displayed. I could see them through the doorway. But the box from Daisy was still in my purse and I fished it out with the slightly crumpled bow leaning to one side.

Mom's eyes lit up even as she spoke. "Fiona Fleming, no presents. You know the rules."

"It's not from me," I said. Hating at that moment her particular ideas about birthdays and fully committing, after seeing just how delighted and excited she was, that next year she'd be getting a present whether she said she liked it or not. "This is from Daisy."

"Oh, how kind." Mom took the box from me, clutched it in her fingers like it was a precious flower. Yup, present rule officially decimated. How had I allowed her to convince me not to give her gifts when she clearly loved them? The paper fell after a long, careful moment she spent pulling the tape free as if the contents were infinitely breakable, the small black and red box stamped with a diamond on the top. She lifted the lid, peeking inside, pulling away the thin layer of cotton while my heart hurt so much

I wanted to hug my mother. And smiled with her at the sight of the slim, silver bracelet with the tiny "Lucy" charm dangling from it.

"Please tell Daisy I'll be along to thank her personally," Mom said. Were those tears in her eyes? "And then to spank her for being naughty. She knows the rules."

I stood, circled the table and hugged my mother, Petunia in the way. She murmured in surprise while I grabbed Dad's chair and pulled it closer, holding Mom's hand. "Thanks for your birthday dinner," I said.

Mom blinked, smiled, beamed. "You're welcome. Will you?" She held out her wrist and the box and a moment later my fingers closed the clasp and the delicate thing dangled from her skin.

"Mom." I sat back, biting my lower lip while she admired her gift.

"Fee." She looked up, face quiet. "Just ask me."

"Where was Dad Thursday night? Was he home?" Of course he was. Stupid question.

Mom didn't answer right away and my heart stopped a beat or two while she sighed and looked down at her hands clasped in the lap of her neat pencil skirt. Her fingers toyed with her name in silver as she spoke.

"I don't know where he was," she said. "But I know what you're implying, Fiona Marie Fleming, and I'm shocked by it." Thing was, she didn't sound shocked.

"What was between Pete and Dad, Mom?" Why did I think, after all this time, either one of my parents had changed? Just because I grew up and moved home, did I really think that was going to mean anything? Secrets. Dad loved protecting his and Mom loved protecting him.

Mom stood, kissed the top of my head. "I know being a detective is in your blood," she whispered into my hair with enough sadness I sagged and didn't fight her. "And though I love your father, Fee, I'm willing to tell you now I think it was a big mistake for John to keep you from pursuing a life in law enforcement." She did? Nice to know Mom might be on my side for once. Not that it really mattered. "You'd be great at it. A chip off the block, as they say." I looked up into her eyes. Pride there, for me. Amazing. "But please, just drop this. I'm asking you to let Crew handle it."

I didn't answer right away, couldn't bring myself to nod or even murmur agreement. Because she was right, I guess. I was too much like Dad.

Mom patted my cheek, the iron finally showing again past her little smile. "Be a good girl and mind your own business," she said from the Fleming family playbook and left the room, sad pug gazing longingly after her.

CHAPTER SIXTEEN

FORGET TRYING TO TALK to Dad, or even find him. I helped Mom with the dishes before bundling up the pug and heading for home, actually grateful to have Petunia beside me even for that short drive. How strange, it had only taken two weeks for her to feel like a necessary part of my life. And for me to forget about Ryan. Well, mostly. I scowled through the windshield as I sped the short distance to the B&B. Thinking about my ex always riled me up, though it was gratifying to realize he wasn't in my thoughts all that often despite the fact we were together for so long. He didn't deserve me, I knew that. After cheating, well, he deserved a solid kick in the privates. But surely that meant I was better off, the fact I didn't linger over him like a tongue pressing into a sore tooth?

Actually put a perk in my emotional state. Independent woman, that was me. Now, if only I could figure out what to do with the mess I was in, I'd be all set. That meant finally taking a solid look at the papers Pete Wilkins dropped in my lap, aversion to them or not.

Not to mention filling in Crew about Simon and Terri and the flower shop. And digging up that mysterious box in my garden. So much fun to be had. All while hopefully avoiding a murder rap. Good times in Reading, Vermont for Fiona Fleming.

The ladies of grim gloom were already gone when I arrived, Daisy rushing forward with her purse over her arm to kiss my cheek.

"Did she love it?" She beamed at me before hurrying past. "Got to run! Big date."

I let her go without an argument, turning to find Petunia sitting in the middle of the foyer still in her harness, staring at me like I'd broken her big, canine heart not giving in and letting her have cheesecake. I sighed and rolled my eyes at her.

"You have tons of food that doesn't give you gas," I said, removing her harness before going to the guest listing on the computer to check up on business. The house felt empty though registration was as full as ever, tourists out and about, I could only imagine. It was a gorgeous night and it made sense they'd be exploring our cute little town.

I scooted downstairs to retrieve the papers before returning to the main floor, Petunia's claws clicking their way behind me while she followed my every move. When I settled on the sofa in the front parlor, she heaved herself up beside me, head in my lap instantly, big brown eyes locked on my face.

She really shouldn't have been on the furniture but I didn't have the heart to tell her that. Instead, I slipped the three wrinkled sheets from the envelope and took a peek. So weird how my heart pounded and then settled while I read over the cover letter—basically telling me what Pete told me, that Grandmother Iris signed Petunia's to him and I had about forty-eight hours to vacate—and then the two page contract in legalese that I struggled to decipher before eyeballing my grandmother's signature on the bottom of the last page. Also signed by Pete and witnessed by someone whose name I couldn't make out.

It was clear though, this paperwork was a photocopy of the original. Of course he'd never give me the document that proved his claim. But I wanted a look at the actual signatures, just to reassure myself this wasn't some hoax. Though, stomach sinking and reality settling in, I sadly accepted the truth was likely something I didn't want to face.

For whatever reason, while in the nursing home for her last days of hospice, Grandmother Iris signed away Petunia's to a total stranger.

Now that Pete was dead, I had to talk to his heir. Getting this sorted out had to be my first priority. And maybe I could make an arrangement with whoever controlled Pete's estate now that he was gone? I was on my feet and moving toward the front door before the groan and thud behind me stopped me in my tracks and I turned to face the unhappy pug.

"You can't come," I said. Winced. "And I can't go, either." No one to watch the place, was there? But the house stood empty and I really needed to take care of this. Did I dare just abandon my post and run off? My stern sense of responsibility kicked in before I could do something so foolish.

And instead did the only thing I could think of. I called my mother. At 7:30 at night. On her birthday. And she came without a second thought, showing up at the front door of the B&B with a beaming smile for me and a kiss for Petunia.

"Thanks, Mom," I said, hurrying past her with Petunia on a lead. Because I was a sucker for a sad dog face. "I'll just be a half hour."

"Don't worry, sweetie," she said, waving from the door as I set a wicked pace Petunia would soon come to regret. "Go run your errands. I'm going to snoop in the kitchen." That would drive Betty nuts if she knew. Mom's laugh made me grin before I hustled off. Because, no, I didn't tell my mother where I was really going. I wasn't an idiot. I lied point blank to the woman who raised me so I could do exactly what she asked me not to.

Mind my own business. As if.

In the time it took for Mom to arrive I'd looked up Pete's address. Just a few blocks away in the wealthiest part of town, so easily walkable. That was, for me. Petunia did her best to keep up, huffing and puffing her little pug heart out, but it was clear by the time we were halfway there this was going to be one of those times I wished I wasn't such a softy.

"Come on, Petunia," I said, tugging on her harness through the retractable lead. "You really need to get more exercise."

She looked up at me, tongue hanging out, and I'm sure she was telling me off in her head. Well, this had been her idea, hadn't it?

I rounded the corner of Wicker Street and looked up the block. Pete Wilkins had purchased the giant house at the end, the grand front entry flanked by trees and hidden partially behind a large gate and fence. But the gate stood open tonight, just my luck, as I half-dragged, half-cajoled the pudgy pug down the sidewalk toward the front door.

I just reached the crosswalk when I spotted a blonde emerging from the side gate and into the street beside the house. Thanks to the mountains, it was already feeling dark though the sky remained blue overhead, but still plenty of light to see by. Younger than me and dressed in a suit that really should have been a size bigger with a bit more cleavage coverage, she looked around as if she wasn't supposed to be there before slipping into the front seat of a beat up little compact car and driving away. Nothing to do with me, but odd just the same as Petunia and I made our way to the front walk and up the cobbled path to the towering main door. Polished wood, dark and carved with detailed leaves and three lead lined panes of glass guarded the interior. The doorbell echoed a booming song within and I flinched at the commanding summons of it. Petunia didn't seem to notice, just grateful, I think, to have a chance to sit and catch her breath.

The door swept open the exact moment the pug farted enthusiastically, the sound and stench about two seconds apart. The woman on the other side of the door stared at me in startled shock and neither of us spoke a long moment while Petunia's flatulence went on for another heartbeat before she groaned her delight and licked her chops, clearly pleased with herself.

Cheese farts. The worst.

"Sorry," I said. "The guests feed her things she shouldn't have." I stuck my hand out and felt the limp response from the black dressed brunette. The same one from the sheriff's office, I realized then, someone I knew I should recognize and now understood why. No wonder Dad didn't want to talk about her. This was Pete Wilkins's wife, Aundrea Patterson. Well, Wilkins. But everyone knew no one really escaped the Patterson name. Reading's most powerful founding family was rather possessive of its members from what I could recall and I doubted she was an exception. "Fiona Fleming."

Her face tightened at my name and she dropped my hand like I'd burned her. "What do you want?"

Not that I was expecting a warm welcome or anything. Her husband died in my koi pond. But I wasn't prepared for the vitriolic antagonism she aimed in my direction. And only then realized, like an utter idiot, it had only been a day since Pete passed and here I was looking for answers to my own problems.

I almost backpedaled out of there, cursing at myself in my head. But the young man appeared, looking enough like Pete around the edges if more his mother in height and build he had to be his son as I fish lipped and stuttered and tried to find an excuse to be there on their front step like the insensitive and heartless woman I obviously was.

"Can we help you?" At least he didn't look like he wanted to wipe me off the bottom of his shoe. I focused on him and plunged.

"Fiona Fleming," I said in a gush. "Your father claimed to have ownership of my bed and breakfast.

I wanted to see the original paperwork so I can talk to my lawyer." Oh, Fee. Fee, Fee, Fee.

The young man's face tightened, arm going around the woman's shoulders. His mother's shoulders. Yes, he looked way more like her than the big man who I'd met once and would despise the rest of my life. Hopefully he took after her in temperament as well and not his father. Unless she was worse than Pete. I couldn't imagine that.

"We haven't even buried my dad yet," he said. "I'm sorry for your business troubles, but I won't be looking at my father's affairs until after the funeral." He stressed those last words until I felt about three inches high and with good reason.

"Great then," I said, smiling like a total goof ball and skin crawling with my own inappropriateness. "Thanks for that. I'll be in touch."

He slammed the door in my face while I sagged and sighed, wishing I was anywhere but there.

CHAPTER SEVENTEEN

NOT ONLY DID I humiliate myself in front of the Wilkins's, we barely made it to the end of the walk when Petunia lay down and refused to walk any further.

"Oh, no you don't," I said. "Up, young lady. We need to get out of here."

But she clearly had her dose of exercise for the day and wasn't going anywhere, her round belly heaving, pathetic pug face turned up to me like I should go on without her because she couldn't make it another step in the falling darkness.

I don't know if you've ever tried to carry a portly pug or not, but let me tell you, it's not a pleasant process. First, she was dead weight, and she wanted to lick me in thanks or to prove her ownership of my clearly pathetic self-esteem. And the *farting*. I can't even talk about the farting. No more cheese for her ever. I think I was stoned on the stench by the time I set her down in the foyer of the B&B, Mom's smile of greeting turning to a faintly disgusted look of shock at my red face and the miasma of smell still lingering.

"Thanks, Mom," I said, sinking to the bottom step of the main staircase to catch my breath.

"Any time, sweetie," she said, easing toward the door while Petunia happily let another one rip. "You really should take her to the vet. I think there's something wrong with her insides."

I glared at Mom as she waved and left, before turning my attention to the stinky pug. "Outside," I snapped, pointing at the kitchen. And followed her out to the back garden. Petunia found a lovely spot in the middle of the path to do her business, looking up at me with her bulging eyes as if holding eye contact was her only lifeline while she extruded a giant pile of brown and orange goo on the walkway.

Done, she grunted and sat next to it, tongue lolling out, like she was proud of her accomplishment. While I fetched the small garden shovel and buried the evidence while doing my best not to throw up.

The only benefit? She chose to have her giant, stinky dump near the crime scene. And that gave me the prompting to use said shovel on the box. First. Because no way was I getting dog poo on it.

Petunia observed with quiet concentration while I uncovered the treasure. The box, rusted and pitted but still solid, bore a newish looking padlock, the twelve inch by six inch by six inch rectangle a little heavy in my hand when I lifted it from the ground and dusted it off. A quick glance around to make sure I was alone and I was hustling down the path to the house and down the steps to my apartment, Petunia clicking her way behind me.

I set it on my kitchen counter, examining the lock. I had no idea what combination to use, the thing reminding me of high school and forgetting the slip of paper with the urgently important numbers on it usually within minutes of closing the hasp. I could just cut it off, but without the proper tool I'd be wasting my time.

The sound of footsteps upstairs and the door opening to laughing guests returning lured me away and it wasn't until I fell into bed later that night I thought again about the odd box on my kitchen island. I stared at it the next morning over a cup of coffee but didn't have time to do a thing about it. Sunday morning loomed and I had a huge day ahead of me.

Did I. Sundays were like Armageddon for businesses in Reading, and Petunia's was no exception. The mass exodus of clientele met the influx of newbies to the point I was grateful to have Daisy there so I wasn't on my own. The foyer, as big as it was, packed with people and luggage going out and coming in, overflowing often into the front sitting room while Petunia wandered between legs and rollies for her goodbye and welcome pets. Both Mary and Betty stayed out of view, bless their old, cold, withered hearts. Not like I could have used the extra hands or anything.

By the time the rooms turned over, me scrambling to change linens and clean bathrooms while Daisy reminded new guests check-in wasn't until 1PM, a rule they ignored anyway, it was after 2:30 and I hadn't had a chance to eat breakfast let alone pee or think or do anything but scrub, fluff and tuck.

Daisy, looking as polished and unruffled as always despite her slightly frantic approach to the morning, sat next to me with a happy sigh and sipped her coffee, helping herself to the tray of sandwiches I placed between us while Betty huffed her silent disdain for our intrusion on her domain. Let her be pissed. We'd just cleared and reloaded the entire B&B without one person losing their temper, including us. The finger sandwiches Betty made for tea were a small price for her to pay.

Daisy nibbled a corner of cream cheese and cucumber, offering a little to Petunia while I groaned but didn't argue. The pug slorped down her portion and looked for more while I took a grateful drink of my own java.

"How was your date last night?" I could at least try to be a friend and show interest in Daisy's life. Kudos to me for remembering she even had a date, right?

She wriggled her narrow butt on her stool, pale pink skirt riding up and her cute little matching sweater tugging at the front when she did. "Just a tourist," she said, rolling her eyes like that meant something. "Free dinner, though."

I loved her attitude, laughed. "So that's your suggestion for a love life around here, huh? Date tourists for the cheap grocery bills?"

Daisy tinkled her own laugh, squeezing my hand. "Trust me," she said, "there's not much selection otherwise. Except that very cute and super dreamy sheriff of ours." She sighed and propped her cleft chin in her palm while I choked on my coffee. "So handsome. And that butt in those jeans."

Yes, I'd thought the same thing. But it was pretty clear Crew Turner and I weren't ever meant to be anything but head butting antagonists. So I was having a hard time thinking about him like that.

That butt. Those jeans. Liar.

I set down my coffee cup, annoyed my hands shook a little. "Well, you can have him," I said, surprised at the level of bitterness in my voice, hating I sounded like I imagined Betty and Mary were in their own heads. "And every other man on the planet."

Daisy's big eyes flew wider. "I didn't know you were gay." She patted my hand. "I shouldn't assume."

Oh, for the love of… "I'm not gay," I said. "Just over men."

She frowned a little, head tilt making her confusion clear. "But that's impossible. Isn't it?"

If only. "Tell my ex that the next time you see him," I said.

She leaned toward me then, all ears. "You never did fill me in on what happened."

It was only then I realized I didn't want to talk about it. Or Crew, or anyone else. And that I really *was* over men, thank you. No, boys. Because that's what they acted like. Even my stubborn, avoiding, frustrating father.

Daisy must have realized I wasn't going to answer, because she let it go with the kind of grace I only wished I had at that moment. "Well, if Crew's not your type, we'll find you someone." She perked. "How about that cute Jared Wilkins?" She hesitated then as if only realizing what she just said while I choked a laugh.

"Is that Pete's son's name?" I rolled my eyes. "Just as soon as he gets over the fact his dad died in my back garden, I'm sure we'll be very happy together. And if he wasn't five years younger than me." If not more.

Daisy shrugged. "Didn't stop Vivian."

Do tell. "How nice for her." Bitter, yup.

"Not like Jared gave her much of a shot, though." Conspiracy was Daisy's favorite. She grinned, tight and wicked. "Besides, he's far too nice to go for anyone as horrible as her."

Nice? Was that true? "Nothing like his dad, then?"

Daisy shook her head, honey hair bouncing. "Not a bit," she said. "In fact, he's super kind, volunteers and gives back to the community all the time. Even sponsored the new soup kitchen. Much more his mom Aundrea than anything." Didn't sound like the Pete I met briefly and hated instantly. "He's been at odds with his father for years. In fact," she gave another chunk of sandwich to Petunia as she spoke, "Jared and Pete had a huge fight the day before he died outside Sammy's Coffee downtown."

They had what? I stared at Daisy who straightened from her snack offering as if she hadn't just dropped another suspect in my lap. Forget the coroner's accidental death ruling. Pete's enemies and possible murderer pool was growing by the second.

"Why didn't you tell Crew that?" It would have possibly deflected the sheriff away from me the morning I found the body. Maybe.

Daisy's face crumpled. "Oh, Fee," she said. "I'm sorry. I should have, shouldn't I? I'll do that right away."

No use in getting angry with her, not now. I shook my head and leaned back, forced a smile.

"It's okay." I felt like the rest of my life was going to be telling Daisy nothing she did was her fault. "I'll fill him in."

Would I. Right after I handed him Simon and Terri's story. Because I was done being the focus of Crew's suspect pool, thank you very much.

CHAPTER EIGHTEEN

I LEFT DAISY IN charge and Petunia behind this time. Refused to look at the pug and her desperate sadness I was abandoning her for the great outdoors. The walk to the sheriff's office gave me the time I needed to sort out what I was going to say. And he was going to listen, was he ever.

I should have known nothing was ever so easy, not for me. I had only just passed through the front door of the station, all indignation and self-righteousness, when I realized there was more going on than maybe I should have known about. Okay, definitely more. Because my dad stood in the main bullpen with Crew beside him, heads together, while Pamela Shard, the reporter who was also editor and manager of the local paper hovered in their threesome, listening carefully. I didn't get a chance to ask what was going on, not when the three then disappeared behind Crew's office door, firmly shut behind them.

I turned to Toby Miller, found her with her head down, resolutely not meeting my eyes, the deputies gone, and only she of my dad's loyalty club to badger with questions. I think she must have known I wasn't going away, because she finally looked up with a sigh and shook her head.

"I can't tell you anything, Fee," Toby said. "So just go home, please."

"I've known you since I was a little girl, Toby," I said, laying on the weight of betrayal and hurt as thick as I could. "And you're going to take that attitude with me, of all people?"

Her mouth worked, her small, lined hands clenching on her desk in front of her. The round logo of the Curtis County Sheriff's Department over her right breast moved up and down quickly, the fleece vest her uniform for as long as I could remember, all four seasons of the year.

"You know your father will be furious with me." She had to try that pleading look, those brown eyes reminding me of Petunia. "I can't, Fee."

"Just tell me what connection Dad had to Pete Wilkins," I said. Wheedling, now. And from the look on her face, the way she glanced at the office door, I was wearing her down.

"Fine. That much won't hurt." Toby leaned toward me, all eager now. Like she'd been dying to spill. Bless her. "John has been investigating Pete Wilkins for years, the two old enemies from school. John's never trusted him and Pete proved to be about as honest as your dad expected." She licked her lips, glancing once more at the silent office. "Fraud, building code violations, you name it, going back decades. All of his projects were under scrutiny, including the ski lodge and golf course." Olivia wouldn't be very happy about that. "But it all fell through just recently. Just before your father retired." Toby leaned away, looking sad. "That's all I can tell you."

It was more than I needed. I knew my father, his stubbornness, his relentless pursuit of justice. What would he do if he failed in an investigation? He would go to any lengths to ensure the law was upheld. But murder? Surely he would never go that far. And why, why would he be at my place with Pete? An accident I could see. Maybe the contractor met Dad there that night to talk about the signature and Dad pushed him and…

And.

"Sheriff Turner called your dad in," Toby said as if unable to help herself, like she hadn't just told me she couldn't say more. "The coroner reexamined the evidence and the bruise on Pete's leg? Happened right before he died. Means he didn't slip on his own. That his fall had help. And that means manslaughter at the least."

She covered her mouth with both hands then, shook her head like she'd said too much at last.

"I need to talk to the sheriff." I looked at the closed door. "I have some information he might be interested in. Suspects."

Toby lurched to her feet, hands reaching for me as she hurried around her desk. I found myself being pushed backward toward the exit, panic on her face.

"Just go, Fee, please." Why was everyone so insistent I stay out of this? You'd think she'd want me to give over evidence. Instead, she seemed worried. "Let the sheriff take care of things."

"Do you mean Dad," I asked, "or Crew?"

Toby hesitated and I knew exactly who she referred to. Because change in guard or not, Dad would always be her sheriff.

So was she protecting him from himself? Seemed likely. And that made me very nervous.

Before Toby could make me leave, the office door opened and Pamela exited, looking angry. Which mean neither of the men gave her the information she was clearly after. I used the distraction, skirting around the office receptionist and hurrying through the swinging door at the low gate that separated the front entry from the bullpen and stormed into the office, slamming the door shut behind me so Toby couldn't stop me.

"I have information," I said, a little breathless as the two men stared at me like I'd taken them both by surprise. Good, maybe they'd listen then. "Do you want it or not?"

Dad met Crew's gaze and the two shrugged.

"Wow," I snapped. "With that kind of enthusiasm a girl could really start to feel like she's wanted."

"Just tell us what you know," Crew said like it caused him great pain to speak.

Would have served them both right if I'd turned around and marched out of there. But Petunia's was on the line, let alone murder being back on the table. I relented, telling them about Simon and Terri before sharing Daisy's recollection of the fight between Jared and Pete. They listened, at least, both frowning by the end of it. But neither mentioned the father/son issue, instead focusing on the flower shop.

"We already know there are other victims," Dad said like I was wasting his time.

"News to me," Crew said, scowling at Dad. "That doesn't mean I'm reopening the case, John."

The two faced off like I wasn't there and again the boy hormone levels rose to a disgusting height.

"The man is dead," Crew said at last. "Let it go. And trust me to handle it." He met my eyes, his unreadable. "Now, if you'll escort your daughter out of my office, I have work to do."

Dad mumbled something that sounded a lot like a curse word before he turned his back on Crew, caught my arm in his hand, and began to drag me away.

"Both of you are to make yourselves available for questioning when I need to talk to you." Crew called after us as I staggered after Dad, just tugging free of him as the new sheriff slammed his own door behind me. I scowled up at my father who glared back before turning and stomping out, still muttering to himself.

Leaving me to toss my hands and stare after him in frustration even as the smiling face of Pamela Shard invaded my personal space. Her crisp, blue suit and white shell made her feel professional enough to be a bit intimidating. Or would have if I wasn't my father's daughter. Not that the fact was going to stop her from trying.

"Fiona Fleming," she said, dark, shark eyes cold, bobbed off brown hair tucked neatly behind her ears in no-nonsense sleek lines. "I have some questions for you."

CHAPTER NINETEEN

LIKE I WAS GOING to talk willingly to a reporter. I pushed past her, ignored her huff of indignation, rushing after my dad. Because he and I really had to talk.

I caught him halfway home, forced to run after him. But I must have shocked him because when I grabbed his arm and turned him around he stopped and stared down at me like he didn't know who I was for a second. So lost in thought, I guess, he gave me the upper hand for probably the first time in my whole life.

"Where were you the night Pete died?" I hissed that question at him, knowing we were out in the open, that anyone could overhear but wanting to take advantage of the situation.

Dad started like I'd slapped him before shutting down. "Fishing with the guys," he said.

At night. In the dark. Right.

"Mom doesn't know where you went." I hit him with that accusation.

Dad turned and started walking again. "Your mother doesn't care where I go," he grumbled, "because she trusts me." He threw that at me. "Unlike my daughter. But I go fishing at the cabin with the guys overnight a lot, Fee. You'd know that if you were here."

He did not just punish me with the fact I moved away after high school. Did *not.*

"Do you really think I killed someone?" Dad turned on me then, adding blow to hurt. "Really, Fee? You think I'm capable?"

"I do," I said. "Under the right circumstances." And I did. Because I knew Dad would do anything for Mom. Anything.

"But these circumstances?" At least he didn't argue.

I hesitated because no, I didn't believe it. Not on purpose. But an accident, manslaughter? In the heat of the moment, anything could happen.

We stared at each other a long moment while I struggled to say anything, while he sagged and absorbed my silence. How fun, hurting each other so deeply on a public street in probably the nosiest town in America. Dad turned at last and headed for home, head down, feet dragging a little while I stood watching him go with my heart in my shoes.

Bad daughter.

That didn't remove my need to find out the truth, though, as sad as that was. And now that Crew was on the warpath for a suspect again, I had to try to sort this out. Okay, no. I didn't. I could go home to the B&B, do as they all were telling me, mind my own business. But Petunia's was at risk, my freedom challenged. And no one was willing to tell me what was going on, not really. So taking matters into my own hands? Yeah, I could do that.

Was doing that. Dad should have known he didn't raise the kind of daughter who did what she was told. Not with his DNA hardwired into me. I stomped home to Petunia's, sorting out my game plan. I couldn't do much about the fight between

Pete and Jared. But there was too much of a coincidence between Grandmother Iris's situation and that of Ranjeet Jacob for me to ignore.

They'd both been old, ill and in care. That pointed to the nursing home, didn't it? I'd been meaning to stop in and pick up the box of odds and ends my grandmother left behind. The perfect excuse to check the place out and see if there was a connection to Pete Wilkins. A long shot, okay. But I had to do something or lose my mind.

My car chugged its reluctance as I drove to my destination, but I refused to stop or turn around or go home and be a good girl. Not like going to the home was against the law or anything. Nor was looking into my own best interest.

I pulled into a spot out front of the low, long building, noting the tasteful landscaping and the fact the pale yellow building was probably overdue for a paint job. The tall sign at the gate said Reading Nursing Care, the logo likely designed in the eighties from the tacky colors and clipart appearance. I slipped out of the driver's seat, clutching my bag to my chest, wondering what I thought I was going to accomplish, really. After all, I couldn't barge in and demand to know if Pete Wilkins had been pressuring old people to sign away their property, could I? I snorted at my own ridiculousness and sighed as I swung the straps over my shoulders, the weight cutting in with a familiarity that brought me back to reality. Seriously, what was I thinking? Yes, I would retrieve Grandmother Iris's things, but I was no detective. Robert had that much right.

I was so focused on beating myself up over even considering I might find answers that I almost bumped into someone exiting the building. I looked up at the last second, the sight of scuffed sneakers skimming up over torn jeans and to the lean, five o'clock shadowed face of a young man who winked at me on the way by. He stank of weed in a cloud that followed him closely and looked a little too skinny for his own good, as if smoking up replaced groceries.

I glanced at him over my shoulder, caught him leering at my ass, and flipped him the bird. He waved jaunty cheer before mounting the motorcycle I'd parked next to and drove off without a helmet. Idiot kid.

Well, I wasn't his mother or anything. And I had my own problems. I jerked on the door, the whoosh of air conditioning and disinfectant making me gag, and entered the building.

The lobby hummed softly with the dull strains of music piped through speakers in the ceiling, rewritten classics made boringly tedious for mass consumption. My shoes squeaked on the old tiles polished to their best shine despite their age, and looked around, feeling a little lost in the dim gray of the industrial feeling space.

An office sign lured me toward it, but not before a perky voice called my name.

"Fiona!" I turned to find Peggy perched on a sofa long in need of new upholstery, Cookie in her lap with her cute, pink bow bobbing from her topknot. A clock ticked its ancient time over their heads, a doddering old man next to her, his thin, slumped body draped in a dressing gown two sizes too big for him, plaid slippers on his narrow feet. She wiped absently at the drool running down the man's chin with a crumpled tissue, Cookie wagging her tail at the sight of me.

"Hi, Peggy." I joined them, smiling down at the old man who looked through me with his watery eyes. He didn't move or speak, just sat there with his loose mouth hanging open while my heart ached for him. How much of him survived in there? Or was his mind off in a better place already?

"What brings you down here today?" Peggy's perky question just made things worse. She didn't even seem to notice her companion wasn't aware of her or the world around him.

"Just picking up my grandmother's things." I glanced at the office door. "Through there?"

She nodded enthusiastically, her faintly blue-tinted roller set dull in the florescent lights. One hand reached out and straighten the cane perched against her knee before it could fall over before returning to pat the old man's hand. I almost asked about it, had never seen her walk with one before, but she was already pointing to the door across the foyer.

"You go talk to Ruth," she said. "She'll fix you right up. There she is, now."

I turned and watched a tall, large woman in a white dress with a stethoscope around her neck exit the office, her giant feet squashed into big sneakers. There was something so familiar about her face, past the chin length bob that did nothing for the blockiness of her features, the faint gloss she wore on her lips as if convention called for it, the way her big hands seemed more suited to construction than nursing. But it was clear her role and I left Peggy to go talk to the grumpy looking woman who glared at me like I was interrupting her perfectly orderly day.

"I'm Fiona Fleming," I said, offering my hand which disappeared into the massive one she extended, the firmness of her shake so violent I was happy to have my fingers back in one piece.

"Ruth Wilkins," she said. And my entire world froze while she frowned down at me.

"Pete's sister?" Had to be.

"Better than being his murderer," she said.

CHAPTER TWENTY

I WASN'T EXPECTING THAT kind of response, considering I'd just found out the looming woman was the victim's relative, though the more I stared up at her the more their powerful resemblance turned me into a stuttering, stammering idiot.

"Mrs. Fleming's things are in the office," Ruth said, brushing past me with the kind of presence a freight train might command, even the lightest touch from her big arm making me feel bruised. "Good day to you, Miss Fleming."

I watched her lumber away, caught Peggy's unhappy frown and head shake and shrugged it off. I had to live in this town and encounters with those who knew Pete—for better or worse—were going to happen. Hopefully the more time between his death and some other scandal would ease the discomfort of being thought of as the primary suspect.

I was dreaming of course. Reading residents had long, long memories.

The office was about as nicely lit as the foyer with the same buzzing, flickering fluorescent lights and the exact old vinyl tile now grayed out and flecked with who knew what. A clunky desk tucked in one corner, ancient gray filing cabinets lining the back wall and a heavy wooden door with a smoked glass pane dominating the top center in the far corner with "Ruth Wilkins, Administrator," etched on it.

So, head nurse and the boss? I nodded to the young woman behind the desk as she blinked at me past her thick glasses, stringy dark hair puddling in unattractive chunks on her narrow shoulders. She picked absently at a cold sore at the corner of her thin mouth while I glanced around. Noting the large photograph of who had to be staff behind her, Ruth's giant form filling the middle of the image with a grimace likely meant to be a smile.

No one else looked happy to be there.

"Can I help you?" The receptionist's voice matched the rest of her, high pitched and rather wheezy. She inhaled from a blue puffer, still staring while I offered a quick smile, feeling like I had, indeed, wasted my time. Well, it was mine to waste, wasn't it?

"I'm here for Iris Fleming's things." Both of my hands clenched at the straps of my purse over my shoulder and I had to force an inhale and relax them before I lost circulation. Why was I so wound up? The smell of this place wasn't helping, nor the awkward encounter with Ruth. And knowing I'd come on an errand that would likely end with a box of old nightgowns and regret made my shoulders sag.

"Right. Just a sec." The young woman stood, tugging at her ugly brown cardigan, the pockets laden to overflowing with used tissues and a box of what looked like breath mints. I glanced away as she shuffled in her practical shoes across the office about as fast as a turtle might hustle to a pile of boxes in the corner near Ruth's office door. Searching for a distraction, I studied the photo behind the desk, recognizing the receptionist where she squashed up against her boss with the most awkward smile I'd ever seen. And spotted a face I hadn't expected.

I knew her, but not personally. That pretty blonde in the second row with the big eyes and unhappy expression. I'd seen her yesterday leaving the Wilkins's house. Sneaking out the side yard and driving off like she didn't want to be noticed.

So she worked here, did she? Well, good for her. This was a small town, after all. People were connected to places and each other in oddly layered ways. Still, I couldn't help my curious mind's pondering as the receptionist shuffled back to the desk and deposited a small cardboard box, sealed shut with a single strip of packing tape, one end flapping loose as if it had been too much effort to fix it. In big, messy capitals, IRIS FLEMING glared back at me from the surface.

"ID please." I fished out my wallet, showed her my New York driver's license which she squinted at a moment before shrugging like it didn't matter anyway. "Sign here." The young woman produced a pen with the end chewed to a flat line, still moist from her mouth, I could only imagine, and a battered clipboard with a sheet of paper clinging under the wobbly clamp. I put my wallet away before accepting the pen from her, scrawling my name as fast as I could, hoping the cold sore she bore wouldn't transfer to my fingers from the pen and planning to douse myself in cleanser from the dispenser on the way out.

I left, heart heavy, two pumps of clear gel making my skin dry out as I rubbed vigorously, using my shoulder to push the glass door wide. There was no sign of Peggy and just as well. I wasn't in the mood to talk to anyone, not with the last worldly possessions of my grandmother from her deathbed tucked under one arm.

I sat in the car a long moment, the box in my lap, staring down at her name and the loose flap of dirty tape and wondered if this was what life came to, in the end. My fingers grasped the tape and jerked, pulling loose most of her name with it when it tore the top of the box's surface free, the flaps popping open. Only then did I realize they'd recycled this box, that someone shipped something innocuous and unimportant in the container that held the last bits and pieces of Iris Fleming.

Fury gave me a pounding headache, instant and overwhelming and I had to fish in my purse for a tissue as tears flowed. I blew my nose for the woman I barely knew and emptied the offending box out onto the passenger's seat, tossing the cardboard in the back so it wouldn't touch Grandmother Iris's things ever again.

I was right about the spare nightgown, the faded slippers. A single hair clip with a butterfly on it, costume jewelry at its finest. My fingers trembled as I touched it and, on impulse, I pinned it in my hair before setting aside the pale pink housecoat and stopped in surprise when a folded letter fell out of the pocket and slid down between the seat and the console. A bit of grunting and swearing and I had the envelope, staring down at it and the crease that divided my father's name in two.

I should have just taken it to him, let him open it. Addressed to him or not, though, I felt closer to Grandmother Iris in that moment than I ever had and my fingers tore open the flap before I could stop myself.

And found myself absorbed in the contents:

Dear John,

You were correct about Pete Wilkins, and in exactly the way you expected. I've heard enough rumors in this place to uncover he is not only a fraud and a liar but he really has been using the elderly as a means to acquire property.

So Grandmother Iris was investigating herself, was she? Even gravely ill and on her death bed. Well, I came by my nosiness honestly.

I suspect many things I can't prove, but you must investigate Ruth Wilkins as well at this juncture. She and her brother have been speaking frequently behind closed doors and I'm certain she is part of his crimes.

That would make sense. I frowned at Grandmother Iris's scribbled handwriting and had to forgive her the messiness. She'd been in a terrible state. Would I even have been able to form a sentence in her condition, post stroke, let alone write an entire letter?

Pete isn't the one acquiring the signatures. Whoever is doing it, I will uncover the truth. But they only target those who have not had their power of attorney removed as you suspected so the sign overs are legal and binding. I will attempt to play dumb and perhaps take the risk of Petunia's if the opportunity presents. If so, I will find a way to tell you in my signature who it is had me sign.

I gasped and looked up, staring out the windshield and shaking. Grandmother Iris knew exactly what she was doing. But, sadly, it sounded like she'd actually signed over Petunia's. I needed another look at what she'd written. Because from the sounds of things the whole case against Pete and his underhanded takeover of property could rest in my grandmother's signature.

For now, be well and be brave, as always.

My love, Mother

I needed to take this letter to Dad. That's why, five minutes later, I parked outside the sheriff's office and carried it inside. And handed it to Crew Turner instead.

Traitor.

CHAPTER TWENTY-ONE

THE HARD, WOODEN CHAIR was about as uncomfortable as I remembered it from a few days ago but this time at least I felt like I had the upper hand. Crew read through the letter a few times while I fidgeted and tried not to demand he run out and investigate not only Pete Wilkins but his sister, Ruth. Instead, my foot bobbing at the end of my crossed legs, I shifted positions about three million times while sighing over and over again.

When Crew finally looked up, he had that pinched, unhappy expression I'd come to discover was his expression of choice. Or maybe it was just with me. That unsettling thought vanished as he leaned back in his own chair, springs creaking, and set the letter in front of him.

"You could have taken this to your dad," he said, soft, subdued.

"I know." I shifted again, but this time out of discomfort I was even here. The fact I had turned coat and brought the evidence to the new sheriff wasn't lost on me. "But Dad isn't in that seat anymore, Crew. You are. And he doesn't have the power to do anything about it." I left that hanging. Hoping, "You do," left unsaid, didn't need to be.

Crew nodded, frown smoothing out. "I do appreciate your faith in me." Irony there, and some sarcasm. "But I'm not sure what I can do with the word of a woman who had suffered a major stroke and was dying in a nursing home when she wrote this."

"Seriously?" I gaped at him, wishing now I had taken the letter to Dad after all and screw this useless excuse for a—

"However." Crew cut me off with one raised index finger. I distinctly disliked him in that instant, so much so the very sight of him made me want to throw something at his handsome face. Mess it up a little. Leave him something to remember me by while I languished in prison for assault.

I sat back, arms crossing over my chest while he seemed to mull things over.

"How much do you know about your father's case against Pete Wilkins?" I wasn't expecting that question and it jerked me out of my sullen anger.

"Nothing," I said. "Feel like filling me in?"

Crew drew a breath before shaking his head. "He never told you anything?"

"You've met John Fleming, right?" I grunted a swear word.

Crew laughed then and I forgot for a moment I was supposed to hate his cowardly guts. Because he had this velvety laugh that had warm edges and the kind of depth that stirred things long left unstirred.

"Fee, I need to be honest." He settled then, rubbing at his face with both hands, looking tired and a bit vulnerable. How refreshing. And made me listen even more than the chance I might find out what the hell was going on. "I've read the information your dad had against Pete. Pretty solid case, for all. But it fell apart because John lost his distance." Crew hesitated. "You're not throwing a hissy fit?"

I rolled my eyes. "Just spit it out."

"Frankly, I'd have reopened the case, gone looking for new evidence. Except Pete Wilkins is dead." He fixed me with that blue eyed gaze. "And to be completely honest you and your father are at the top of my suspect list. Well, John, anyway."

I opened my mouth to protest but Crew shook his head and stood, coming to my side, taking my hand and pulling me to my feet. I was acutely aware of how close I stood to him then, of the scent of the aftershave he wore, the fact he used the same laundry detergent as we did at Petunia's. And that he really, really was delicious.

"I don't think you killed Pete," he said, voice low and deep. "But I need to cover all my bases. Okay?"

"You think Dad did it." Well, wasn't I moving and shaking along the same lines? Guilty, guilty, guilty.

"I think I'm going to thank you for bringing evidence to my attention and get back to my job." He grasped me lightly by the upper arm and guided me to his office door. I let him, knowing it was foolish to try to push him at this point. And that if I was going to get anywhere proving Dad didn't kill Pete I had to do it on my own.

Crew must have sensed where my thoughts were or just guessed I wasn't done because he looked down into my eyes, his own full of sincerity and all my resentment toward him leaked out of me.

"I've asked you to stay out of this," he said, "and I know now that's not going to work. But Fiona, if you get hurt because you're poking around in things that aren't your problem, your father will kill me."

I shrugged. "Then you two stop being idiots to each other and find out who killed Pete."

I left then, feeling a bit like I'd won a victory, positive of one thing. If my dad did do it, I'd be the first to know. Because no way was I stopping now.

It wasn't hard to become so absorbed in my next steps I barely remembered driving back to the B&B, nor parking my car in the driveway or even entering the foyer. But the sight of Daisy flapping her hands at me, eyes wide and cheeks pale but for two bright pink points caught my attention and pulled me out of my thoughts quickly enough.

Petunia joined us as Daisy hurried to me and whispered in my ear, the pug sitting firmly on the toes of my shoes.

"I couldn't make her leave," my old bestie whispered loud enough I'm sure they heard her upstairs. "I'm sorry."

I glanced in the sitting room as she gestured with what I'm sure was meant to be a subtle motion but looked like frantic flailing. And found Pamela Shard sitting on the old fashioned sofa smiling at me.

"Miss Fleming," the newspaper woman said. "I've been waiting for you."

CHAPTER TWENTY-TWO

SHE DIDN'T RISE OR try to pursue me and she didn't have to. Small town. I could run and maybe try to hide, but eventually I'd have to face her. With a small sigh I shuffled out from under Petunia's warm butt and entered the room, offering my hand.

"I'm not going to tell you anything," I said with a smile.

Pamela laughed while Petunia grunted her way onto the sofa next to her. The fact the well-dressed reporter took the time to scratch the pug under the chin and behind her ears was at least proof she had a heart buried under there. I sank into the chair opposite while my visitor leaned toward me, hands now clasped before her, dark blue suited elbows on her skirted knees.

"Why don't I talk then," she said, brown eyes on the amber side in the light from the tall windows. "About the fact you no longer own Petunia's."

I couldn't breathe, couldn't speak. She went on while I struggled to survive.

"I know all about it," Pamela said. "I've been working on an exposé about the whole sordid and horrible affair. Legal, despite the lack of ethics behind it." She winced then as if wanting to say more before she jabbed one finger in my direction and sat back to pat Petunia, her tone turning from smug confidence to a hint of compassion. "Your grandmother was a great woman, Fee. I knew her for a long time. And I always trusted her judgment." She held my eyes. "She told me she wrote your father a letter about what she'd uncovered, that Pete Wilkins had accomplices." She said his name as if she had her own axe to grind with him. "But she died before I could find out who was part of it."

"Ruth, she thought." I shook my head, looked away. Didn't matter what I said now.

"You read the letter?" Pamela's hopes spiked and then clearly fell as she sighed. "So no evidence."

I shrugged, paused. "Maybe," I said. And made a decision to trust her with the last bit I hadn't shared with Crew. "I'll be right back."

Less than a minute later the two of us sat, Petunia between us, on the sofa in the front room, staring intently at Grandmother Iris's signature. "She said it would be here." Frustrating, not knowing what I was looking for. It just looked like her name to me.

"This is wrong." Pamela shook her head, squinting at the line of scrawl. "This isn't Iris's normal signature."

Well, there was that. "She had a stroke. That might have changed her handwriting." A long shot. "Could I use that to contest the sign over?" Maybe it wasn't her writing after all? Come to think of it, the more I looked at it, the more I realized Pamela was likely right. This signature lacked the kind of shaky unsteadiness that marked the handwriting from the letter I'd given to Crew. No way did Grandmother Iris's palsy steady so she could sign so cleanly.

"Possibly." Pamela sat back with a sigh. "Certainly makes things interesting from a legal point of view. Except, Fee, I think this proves your grandmother *didn't* get to sign. Or finger the person who actually gained the signatures. Because stroke or no stroke, she would have followed through with her word, especially to John."

"Personally, I'm okay with that," I said. "If it means Petunia's is still legally mine."

Pamela nodded then, faint smile unhappy. "There is that blessing," she said. "The only trouble is all the other victims aren't so lucky." Why did she sound like she took that personally? If I'd learned anything, everyone in this town had something to hide.

"How many victims?" Dad must know. But Pamela was here to ask.

"I've tracked down over twenty," she said. "All out of state, and not one of them willing to contest the signatures. Even the three out of town lawyers I spoke to said the paperwork was legal." She paused then, looking a little embarrassed. "If your grandmother's wasn't, what changed?" Good question. "I meant to bring all of this to your father despite the consequences." Her eyes flickered to me when she said it, pushed on like I wasn't supposed to pay attention to her slip or ask her what she meant about consequences exactly. I let her have her subterfuge. "And then he retired when Iris died and I just don't trust the new boy yet."

That made two of us. Or did it?

"So we both agree there's a loose thread here," I said. "If Pete was targeting out of towners to ensure no one found out, why change that now? Mr. Jacob was pretty well known around here. Surely Pete would expect someone to find out he was taking advantage of a local. And to go after Grandmother Iris after Dad had a case built against him…"

"But your father's case fell apart," Pamela said. "For reasons I believe had nothing to do with John's police work, no matter what Crew Turner says."

Loyalty to my dad made me agree. "Still, you're right. I'm thinking whoever Pete has on the inside acquiring the signatures has their own agenda now. For whatever reason."

"Ruth?" It made the most sense.

"Indeed." Pamela stared at the paperwork in her lap. "As for the Jacob's, well, I had thought Simon was into other things. And perhaps that's kept him silent." She flinched then as if she'd said more than she wanted.

"Like?" Yeah, worth a shot.

She just smiled then. "I can take this to my lawyer friends if you want. Compare the signatures." She seemed eager now. As if she'd been waiting a long time to be able to act.

I shook my head, taking the papers back from her while she sighed her disappointment. "Now that I have reason to suspect this isn't Grandmother Iris's handwriting, I can take it from here." I had more I could tell her, but did I dare? Instead, I went fishing. "For all we know, it was Aundrea Wilkins, the wife, who helped him with this." That was logical too, wasn't it?

The look of sheer shock and skepticism on Pamela's face made me pause. So, was she instead maybe the reporter's source? Part of the consequences she mentioned? That would make sense, especially since Pamela lurched to her feet and offered her hand, suddenly in a hurry to get away from me.

Bullseye.

"Thank you for your trust in me," Pamela said, handing me her card. "I'll be in touch. Fee." She paused one more moment, hand squeezing mine. "I'm here to help."

I watched her go, hugging the papers and her information to my chest while my mind churned. Suddenly the interior of the B&B was just too much for me. I lurched for the front door, needing air, Petunia pattering along beside me. When I paused to look down into her face, I sighed as she hooked me with those brown eyes.

"Fine," I grumbled, reaching for her harness hanging by the door. "But I'm not carrying you this time."

She grunted her agreement. Such a liar.

Five minutes later, while I stared across the street at the front door of Jacob's Flowers and considered my course of conversation with Terri, I hesitated. It was Simon I needed to talk to. He'd been the reticent one. But would he tell me what happened? His wife seemed to be in the dark about what really went down. What kind of deal did Simon strike with Pete Wilkins to keep the flower shop? Or, like Grandmother Iris, did he uncover the signature was a fake?

I was about to cross, a small pack of tourists brushing by me with their cell phones snapping endless pictures, when I spotted the alley door of Jacob's pop open and Simon exit. He looked around as if hoping no one would see him in the afternoon bustle before disappearing down the alley into the next street over.

Impulse moved my feet, hurrying me across the asphalt with a wave for the car that pulled to a stop to let us go by, Petunia huffing along beside me. Because dragging a lazy pug along while I followed a suspect was about as sneaky as I got.

CHAPTER TWENTY-THREE

SIMON WAS IN A hurry and I did end up hefting Petunia a time or two so I could keep up. I was sweaty and frustrated by the time we reached the other side of town, about ten blocks of swearing at the pug for not being more athletic and waving off the occasional dog fart.

I almost lost Simon twice, though Reading was small enough it was easy to take a side street and catch up again. He wasn't exactly trying to hide his movements, but he kept his head down and seemed like he was a man on a mission. I had no idea why it felt important to follow him, except I guess I was just so frustrated by my lack of answers and all the questions hanging around me a bit of an adventure—

fruitless and a waste of time or not—made me feel like I was at least accomplishing something.

When he crossed the street at the end of the block, heading for a small, seedy spot, I grunted and set Petunia down, pissed at myself for the whole waste of time. A bar. So he was a drinker, big deal. I'd hustled all this way just to watch Simon Jacob have a beer.

Except he didn't go to the front door of The Orange with its aptly painted entrance. Instead, he entered the side alley. I eased my way down the street and kept an eye on him, watching as he paused next to a young man loitering in the narrow way. And started. I knew that kid, had almost bumped into him at the nursing home. The two spoke for a moment, something changing hands. And then, without further conversation, Simon knocked on a side door that swung open a moment later, the dull gray hiding whoever stood behind it and let him in.

I watched a long time but nothing else happened. Dozens of scenarios crossed my mind, but the most obvious had to be the truth. I'd seen enough drug exchanges on the streets of New York to know one when I saw one. No, I'd never made a buy myself. Not that I was uninitiated. Ryan and his friends had enough weed around I got stoned some nights just from breathing the air in the living room. But it wasn't my thing, not by a long shot. Not with a sheriff for a father, though I'm sure some would think rebellion would drive me in that direction.

Pamela mentioned Simon was into other things. This was clearly one of them.

But there was no way of knowing for sure unless I talked to the young man who made the supposed sale. Hand firm on Petunia's leash, knowing it was stupid and likely dangerous, I gathered my nerve and inhaled to take a step forward. Just as the small econobox pulled up and the blonde girl from the Wilkins's house got out.

The same girl from the staff photo at the nursing home.

I held still, Petunia happy to be sitting tight, and watched as the young woman spoke to the young man with her head close to his and an unhappy expression on her face. I don't think, in retrospect, I could have been more obvious, staring at them the way I did and with really no excuse to be standing there for so long if I wasn't spying. But neither seemed to notice me, carrying on a heated conversation far too quiet for me to make out over the infrequent cars that drove past. The girl then turned her back on the young man and climbed into her car, driving away while he lit a cigarette and looked up, meeting my eyes.

I hurried away, dragging Petunia behind me, kneejerk reaction to being caught. But something was clearly going on and I intended to find out what.

I stopped in to my parent's house on the way home on impulse. I really had to talk to Dad, even if he wasn't telling me anything himself. Mom greeted Petunia with a kiss for her squish face, a bowl of water after tsking at me for letting the poor beast get dehydrated—I'd carried her most of the way, so I was the thirsty one, but whatever—and a banana all to herself.

"John's not here," Mom said, the last of the mushy fruit disappearing down the dog's throat while she pathetically gazed at my mother like she was starving and wouldn't she share just one more bite?

Of course he wasn't. That would be too easy. "Where is he?" I felt like I had proverbial ants in my pants. I needed to dump what I'd seen and Dad was the only person I could think of who might do something about it, sheriff anymore or not.

"The pub," Mom said with her long suffering forced joviality. "With the boys. Probably playing darts."

I thought of The Orange and its—no pun intended—seedy appearance. But that wasn't Dad's hangout. The Harp and Thorn was an Irish rip off the locals called authentic where the old boys liked to hang out. I scooted home, left Petunia in Daisy's tender care and immediately headed for the pub in question.

Talk about a tourist haven, from the excessively Tudor exterior to the high ceilings and all wood interior, the giant bar and the girls dressed in green. I spotted a few gents in the back tossing darts, but not the hulking form of my dad.

A quick inquiry with the bartender gave me a chill.

"Haven't seen John all day," Patrick Huss said, slurring slightly, his hazel eyes watery, red veins standing out on his nose. Sampling the wares a bit too much, was he? Not my problem. He owned the place, so if he wanted to drink his profits that was his business, quite literally. And the fact he'd been a bit of a booze hound in high school didn't make this realization a stretch.

It was a long, slow walk despite only being a few blocks to the B&B while I pondered the truth. Dad told Mom he was at the pub. Dad wasn't at the pub. Dad told me the night Pete died he'd gone fishing with the guys. If I cornered any of them, would they give me the same story? Or was he lying about that, too?

The sullen Jones ladies of Petunia's were gone when I arrived back, and just as well. I hadn't had much in the way of conversation with either of them the last few days, both of them with their heads down doing their work and staying out of my path. Fair enough. Seemed love wasn't lost in either direction.

Daisy fled as soon as I gave her the go ahead, waving at me and blowing a kiss for Petunia whose farts now distinctly smelled of bananas. An improvement, I guess. I fed her dinner, fielding a few calls from new visitors and stocking up a guest or two with towels and—what was wrong with these people and their digestive systems?—toilet paper before retiring with a cup of coffee in the back garden to think.

I didn't get to sit on the white wicker bench in the far corner and enjoy my drink. Not when I spotted someone poking around, a distinctive someone who had absolutely no business being in my place.

CHAPTER TWENTY-FOUR

MY COFFEE MUG SPILLED sideways as I slammed it down on the side table and huffed my way to the koi pond where Vivian French peered into the water like she'd find the answers I'd been looking for.

"Vivian." She squealed and spun at the sound of my voice. One high heel stuck in the soil, digging a big hole as she turned and jerked her foot free, shaking mud from her shoe with a look of disgust. "What are you doing here?"

"Fee." She clasped one manicured hand to her chest, fluttering her fake lashes at me while she tossed her ice blonde hair. Today's outfit consisted of a pale pink suit that fit her like it was made for her and brought out the faint tan of her skin. "I brought the bread order, didn't Daisy tell you?"

That sickly sweet tone told me she'd done nothing of the kind and was only here to satisfy her morbid curiosity. Petunia, meanwhile, chose that exact moment to do something she never, ever did. With a soft grunt and a fart of epic proportions, she stood up on her hind legs and pawed at the front of Vivian's suit. Two long, dirty paw prints stretched down the length of her skirt, claws hooking into the knee of Vivian's hose and tearing a giant hole in her stockings before the pug landed on all fours again with a satisfied groan.

"BEAST!" Vivian vainly swiped at the muddy prints, making a bigger mess than Petunia had. I almost laughed, so very close. The dog knew better. Grandmother Iris trained her pugs to stay down off the guests, to be polite and quiet and endearing to everyone. For whatever reason, Madam Petunia the Fourth either lost her mind for a moment or felt exactly the same about our unwelcome visitor as I did.

"What a shame," I said. "Guess you should run along home and change."

"This is a Grace Fiore suit," Vivian snarled.

"And this is my property," I shot back. "Since I don't recall inviting you, you can leave. Now."

Vivian's eyes narrowed, nasty smile pulling at her overly full lips. "That's not what I heard," she said, hissing spite putting a snake to shame. "Maybe I need to talk to Jared about acquiring this dump from him. So I can bulldoze it and turn it into a respectable hotel."

How the hell did she…?

Vivian's expression turned to delighted disdain. "Word gets around, dear Fanny," she said, flicking her fingers at me.

It wouldn't have taken much, just a quick shove, really. A lurch forward and two hands on her shoulders and she'd be in the pond. That thought froze me in place. Was that how Dad felt? When he pushed Pete? But no, I didn't know for sure it was my father, did I? So, the killer, manslaughter or premeditated or whatever. Yes, it would be that easy.

I'm not sure what came across my face that made Vivian seem suddenly so uncomfortable but instead of continuing to prod me she paled and eased sideways onto the path, her dirty high heel trailing mud onto the stones. I looked down to find my hands in fists at my sides, Petunia staring up at me in studied silence, and figured I had to look like I'd killed Pete Wilkins with my bare hands.

Probably not the best expression to have on my face at that moment, not when a familiar voice interrupted.

"Ladies." Crew appeared beside me, frowning at me before nodding quickly to Vivian.

Her face instantly brightened, her fear gone, a look of proprietary hunger crossing over her before she settled on that prom queen perfection she'd managed to cultivate since childhood.

"Crew." There was the eyelash flutter again, the sultry tone of voice, the hip cock despite her dirty state. "How lovely to see you."

"Vivian." I fought a smirk at how uncomfortable he sounded all of a sudden. "How are you?"

Small talk? So there was something between them, but it didn't end well. Or was still devolving, at least in his estimation if not hers.

"You didn't call me last night." Her duck lips made her look more ridiculous despite the clear attempt to make him feel guilty for breaking her heart. "You promised."

"I've been busy with the case." Why did he look guilty when he met my eyes? So they were dating.

"You still owe me a dinner," Vivian said. "I've been ever so patient."

Ah, the truth came out at last. No date, but she wasn't quitting. Fascinating, in a stomach clenching kind of way. And about as much as I was willing to take.

"Vivian was just leaving." I turned my body sideways, gesturing for the kitchen door. She glared at me as if I'd interrupted her best laid plans before deciding she'd lost this round and tossing her head one last time.

"I'll be back," she said to me, teeth vicious in her grin. "With Jared. Crew." Amazing how she could shift herself like that, from pit viper to alluring seductress faster than I could take a breath. But she managed it somehow before drifting past, backside swaying in a way that was likely meant to keep Crew's attention. And when I glanced his way, I sighed to find she'd done her job there, at least.

He flinched when she disappeared and caught me watching him. "She's…"

"A pain in the ass and not someone you want to trust." I strode past him for the kitchen door, checking to make sure she'd really left and wasn't snooping around. Nope, from the sound of her car driving off she'd really gone. Good.

Crew followed me inside, the ticking of Petunia's claws hiding the sound of his footsteps. I was halfway downstairs to my apartment before I froze, remembering the box on my kitchen counter. The very box I'd dug up from the crime scene and hadn't told him about. Crew bumped into me with a soft sound of surprise before I sprinted the rest of the way down and hopped up on the counter, my butt hiding the box which I tucked ungracefully into a nook, sliding a bowl of fruit to one side to shield the rest of the view.

Crew's frown of concern was more this chick is nuts than she's hiding something, so I took that as a win.

"You're here for a reason?" I'd just seen him not so long ago. Petunia sat at my feet, looking back and forth between us as Crew sat on a stool and shrugged, elbows on the counter, muscular forearms showing where he'd rolled up the sleeves of his tan uniform shirt. He had a tattoo on his right wrist, looked like an anchor and a skull. How interesting. And irrelevant.

"I did my best," he said, "but I figured after you came to me today I should at least warn you."

That didn't sound good. "Of?" Hiding the box was silly, really. He had no proof I dug it up from the back garden. And there could be something waiting in there that might help the case. Grandmother Iris had proven a smart cookie. Should I just pull it out and get him to help me open it?

"State troopers are getting involved." That froze me in place and all thoughts of sharing went out the window. "Because of your father's old investigation, they've decided they need to look into Pete's death personally."

Was that a bad thing?

"Fiona." Crew swallowed. "If either of you had anything to do with the murder I can't protect you."

Silence for a moment while I processed that. So, he really did think Dad killed Pete. A trained investigator, a sheriff. Thought Dad was a murderer. The same thing that had been bouncing around with increasing difficulty to ignore in my own head.

"We don't need your protection," I said with as much conviction as I could muster. "Because neither of us had anything to do with it."

Crew's mouth opened and for a long time he looked like he was going to protest. And then he shrugged and stood like this was my last chance to come good and he'd been disappointed by my lack of admission of guilt.

"They'll be here midweek," he said. And left. While the corner of Grandmother Iris's strange metal box dug into my butt and I wondered if Crew would offer Dad the same warning he just handed me.

CHAPTER TWENTY-FIVE

I SAT ON THE counter for a good five minutes after Crew had gone, pondering my next steps. When I slid forward and hit the tile, I turned and pulled the box toward me, staring down at the padlock, fingers running over the pitted metal of the rectangle. I tried a few combinations, absent and not believing their usability. My birthday, Dad's, Mom's. Even Grandmother Iris's. Nothing. And still without the means to break the lock.

I carried it into my bedroom, tucking it under the bed, sinking to the quilt. Whatever the box contained, I had other things to think about right now.

It was an uneasy night's sleep and a bleary cup of coffee endured with sideways stares from Mary and Betty while they served breakfast in the main dining room the next morning—a bright and sunny Monday—before I actually admitted to myself there was a real possibility Dad was in a lot of trouble. And while there was a chance something else was behind Pete's death, I couldn't help but go back to the property acquisitions through unethical means as the reason for the contractor's murder. I needed to see the original document, the one my grandmother supposedly signed, with a copy of her actual signature in my hands for comparison.

But Jared wouldn't talk to me, nor would his mother, Aundrea. The funeral hadn't happened yet and might be put off for some time if the state troopers had their own investigation to do. That meant going to the source myself.

The audacity of the idea appealed to me. As soon as breakfast was over, the guests out and about for the day, I left Daisy to man the phones and, leaving unhappy Petunia behind as well, stuffed the photocopy of the paperwork and an old signed letter from my grandmother into my purse and hit the sidewalk.

Pete's office was just down the block from the coffee shop where Daisy claimed to have witnessed the two Wilkins's having a fight. I stopped in to chat with the baristas at Sammy's Coffee, but neither of the girls working had any recollection of the argument and it was busy enough at the counter I was quickly aware I wasn't welcome if I didn't have an order to place.

The late morning sunshine was at distinct odds with my mood while I paused outside Sammy's and stared across the street at Wilkins Construction Inc. Jaw about as set as my determination, I strode forcefully to the glass door and jerked it open, stepping into the air conditioning with battle in mind.

Only to stop and stare at the blonde girl from the Wilkins's house, the same girl in the staff photo at the nursing home. The very girl who seemed to know the supposed drug dealer working beside The Orange. Too many links and crossovers to be small town coincidence.

She stared at me in shock, like she knew me, face paling out except for some red blotches that traveled down her throat and into her cleavage. She dressed a lot like a professional girl who didn't understand propriety very well, or understood it on the other end of professional, if you know what I mean. Suit a bit too tight, shirt unbuttoned one too many, skirt needing two or three inches to be really office worthy. But there was an innocence to her that didn't raise my hackles, instead calming me and giving me confidence here was someone who had information I could use.

"Fiona Fleming," I said, sticking out my hand with a real smile.

She hesitated before taking it, but when she shook it her grip was firm and authentic. "Alicia Conway," she said. "What can I do for you?"

"I'm looking for paperwork Mr. Wilkins had in his possession, supposedly signed by my grandmother." I pulled the copies out to show the girl who took them and nodded, swallowing hard. She suddenly seemed nervous and didn't act surprised, handing them back after barely a glance.

"Petunia's," she said. "Yes."

So, she was in on this whole thing? I found that hard to believe, not with the way she seemed upset by my presence but not guilty. Just sad.

"You work at the nursing home." I didn't frame it as a question. Let Alicia think I knew far more than I did.

She gulped, shrugged. “I used to,” she said. “Pete—Mr. Wilkins—hired me three months ago to be his personal assistant.” She tugged at the hem of her skirt like the length wasn’t her idea. I’d despised him pretty much right away but knowing he’d bullied this girl into the kind of clothes she wore made me all the more nauseated.

“Did you know what your boss was up to?” I tucked the papers back into my bag, leaving that open question hanging between us.

Alicia shook her head, blonde curls trembling, color flooding her face to her perfectly drawn eyebrows. “I don’t know what you’re talking about.”

“But you said you did,” I said. “Petunia’s.”

She hesitated, clamped her lips shut. “Please,” she whispered. “I can’t help you.”

Frustrated irritation cut through my kindness and even knowing I was suddenly playing the bully didn’t stop me. “I need to know what’s going on.”

Alicia shook her head again, a quick movement, eyes averted. “I’m sorry.”

Well, it wasn’t like I could beat information out of her or anything. Could I? Sigh. But I could try a threat. “If I find out you were part of this—”

She gasped softly, face falling, sorrow returned. It was a long time before she spoke, hands clasping her elbows as if that grip was all she had to hold herself together.

"Pete didn't keep any important papers here," she said, voice shaking and just loud enough to hear. She looked up, eyes catching mine, hers full of tears, long lashes thick with mascara sticking together thanks to the heavy moisture. "If you want to find what you're looking for, check the site trailer at the equestrian center he was building. Near Carter's Creek." She licked her lips. "That's all I know."

I could have prodded her further, but Alicia gave me more than anyone I'd talked to so far. And the poor girl really looked like she'd just put herself in genuine danger.

"Thank you," I said, pulling back on the mean girl attitude. "Are you okay?"

Alicia sobbed once, wiped at her nose with a shaking hand. "If you leave."

Okay then. "Call the sheriff if you're in trouble." It was the best I could do if she wouldn't take help from me. "Alicia." If Ruth was involved as Grandmother Iris suggested in her letter, was she threatening the girl?

She bobbed a nod before laughing softly. "You have no idea."

Maybe I shouldn't have left her there. Whatever trouble she was in, she'd likely put herself in it. That didn't mean I should be heartless or care less about her. But if she wasn't willing to help herself… still, maybe she was trying, giving me the directions she did. One more person to worry about.

I exited the office, back into the rising heat of the July day, and looked up to spot the last person I expected hustling past on the other side of the street. And followed Simon Jacob, knowing where he was going, unburdened with a pug this time and determined to tie up his particular part of the puzzle one way or another.

CHAPTER TWENTY-SIX

WHY WAS I NOT surprised we ended up back at The Orange? I did a bit better job hiding my intentions this time, tucking in beside a waste barrel and a light post, watching Simon repeat his routine. The young man was in the same place and after a brief conversation and exchange of what I assumed was money for goods, my quarry knocked on the gray side door and was again admitted without preamble.

Knowing it was probably a stupid thing to do but not really having much impulse control around this whole situation, I drew a breath and crossed the street, smiling at the young man who instinctively smiled back. He straightened from his crouch, cigarette burning between his lips, leering at me as he had at the nursing home.

I waved in greeting, pausing next to him in the dim alley, sunlight missing the mark thanks to the three story buildings surrounding us. I felt like I was in some bad movie making a clandestine buy while, at any point now, the police would show up and arrest me for a variety of illegal acts.

Instead, to the sound of traffic easing by and someone's dog barking in the distance, I inhaled the faintly rotten scent from the dumpster at the end of the alley while the young man winked at me.

"You in the market?" He didn't move other than to look me up and down. The tight t-shirt I wore over my knee length running pants wasn't exactly a fashion statement but he wasn't complaining about the view. Creeped out by this junior taking a long, hard look, I fought to keep my friendly smile.

"Sure am," I said, a bit too brightly, wincing inwardly at my nerdy response. His eyebrow leaped, grin tightening. At least I hadn't scared him off. "Sorry," I went for pathetic, glancing around nervously. "I haven't done this before."

He unwound from where he leaned against the wall, skinny and cocky and trying to look dangerous while a giggle tickled the back of my throat. He couldn't have been more than nineteen, the punk. I was enough my father's daughter the idea of running him in for selling was at the top of my mind when he spoke.

"Well, Pitch is your man, gorgeous," he said, yellow teeth flashing as he smiled, dropping his still burning butt to the ground and stepping on it carefully with the toe of his dirty sneaker. "Saw you lurking yesterday, figured you'd be back for a buy." He coughed a laugh around the exhale of smoke from his final drag. "You middle class ladies just need to ask and I got what you're looking for."

I wondered if he was either inexperienced enough to trust a stranger or if I really was that vanilla I didn't seem to be a threat. Yeah, probably the latter.

"Let me guess," he said, easing closer, eyes on my chest. "You're not here for the happy plant, right? More a vike kind of girl? Or a bit of the old cotton got you going?" He tugged at the back pocket of his jeans. "I got the kicker you're looking for, if that's your speed, sweetness."

I had no idea what he was talking about, but when he produced a little baggie full of what looked like prescription pills, my mind stuttered to a halt before zooming into fast forward. Making all kinds of connections. To nurses and nursing homes and young men who had access to pills they shouldn't have.

And realized maybe this whole thing had a far bigger ream of implications than signatures and property acquisition.

Whatever his instincts, it seemed I'd finally triggered them. Gaping at his stash couldn't have helped because it only took him a second to disappear the baggie before backing away from me, smile fading, frown appearing.

"Wait, you're right." I had lost him, desperation making me stupid. More stupid. Stupider? Whatever. "Please, don't leave."

He shook his head, hands in his pockets, scowling now like a dog preparing to bite. "Beat it, lady," he said. Sniffed the air. "You smell like pork."

"Just tell me what Simon was buying." The young man who called himself Pitch leaned against the wall, looked away.

"I'm just standing here having a smoke," he said, the butt on the ground still emitting a thin trail into the air. "Get lost." He jerked forward then, spun from me. "On second thought, I'm outta here."

I watched him go, frustration and annoyance winning. When I turned around to go back to the street, I stopped dead and stared at Vivian, her little red convertible parked at the end of the alley. Met her narrowed eyes and took in her sudden grin of glee as she waved her phone at me. And then drove off like she'd won the lottery.

Whatever Vivian was up to, that was her problem. Right now, I had another issue to deal with. No Pitch to tell me what Simon was doing here. Which meant I had to go into the bar, right?

I seemed to be on a do all the stupid things roll today, so why not?

Without thinking straight or even really considering anything aside from bubbling irritation, I knocked on the gray door and waited. It swung open, a big man in a suit with a buzz cut and a clear plastic wire running from his ear into the collar of his white shirt looked down at me with a frown to match his bad boy appearance.

"Yeah?" His voice sounded like he gargled cheap whiskey for a living.

"I'm here for Simon." I had no idea what prompted me to say that, but it made the man grin for an instant.

"He just got here. In the back, as usual. You bring the bankroll?" He eyed my outfit.

I didn't comment, not sure what to say. Sure he was going to send me packing. But instead of chasing me off, he stepped aside and waited for me to enter.

Some security. Again, I guess I must have appeared innocent enough if he let me pass. Pretty dumb of me to feel insulted by that, right? I was a badass. In a t-shirt and running shoes and a ponytail of dark red hair. Yeah, such a threat to big, tall and looming.

I walked past him. So, had Simon promised something he couldn't deliver? Blamed it on Terri, maybe. My mind flickered to Vivian. What had she been doing out front? Was she part of whatever this was? Didn't matter now, not really. Whatever the case, I'd strolled into the lion's den and now I could either beg him to let me out again or pretend I knew exactly what I was doing.

Guess which one I picked?

I made it about ten feet to a half open door with a table on the other side, crowded with men and the sound of poker chips being clicked together, a sound I knew well enough from my own days of playing. I could spot an illegal game when I saw it, had taken part in a few back in New York. But was shocked to find one here.

So much so I froze in full sight of the players. And found myself surrounded by a trio of big boys that told me whoever owned this place had a matched set of bullies to do his bidding.

"And who, exactly," a voice said, faint threat in the lilt of his Irish accent, "are you?"

It was that moment I realized I was in a lot of trouble that had absolutely nothing to do with Pete.

CHAPTER TWENTY-SEVEN

THE DARK INTERIOR OF this bar felt about as authentically Irish as The Harp and Thorn screamed tourist attraction. Gone were the sparkly mirrors and the white painted walls, the big screen TV's and the tall ceilings. Instead, this place felt like traveling to the Emerald Isle as I'd had the good fortune to do, though frankly I would have preferred to not feel like I'd fallen into the dark and much worn den of the Irish mob here in Reading, Vermont.

Because that's exactly what I'd done, from the handsome, if older, man in the black t-shirt and jeans, his lean body tight with muscle, gray hair left long and wavy around his square-jawed face. Traces of old, faded freckles and green eyes that matched mine watched me with careful caution as I was seated by a pair of bullies—the hands on my shoulders bigger than the parts of me they grasped—with gentle if insistent pressure.

I sank into the heavy wooden chair at the low table and swallowed my fear, hands tightly clasped in my lap while the man before me observed me with those piercing eyes.

"You look familiar," he said in that accent that did nothing to make me feel more at ease. Though he sat with the kind of relaxed confidence that said any kind of smart mouthing might get me deeper into trouble than I could get myself out of. "But I don't know from where."

"I own Petunia's," I said with more haste than I intended. "The B&B on Booker Street?"

"Ah!" He perked immediately, a huge smile crossing his face while he leaned forward and saluted me with his beer. "Iris's kin. And John Fleming's daughter, I dare say."

Why did the atmosphere suddenly lighten? Things shifted from cut the air with a knife—quite literally—to jovial humor as the man before me nodded with good nature. "You must be Fiona. Fee, aye? Good Irish name for a lass." He seemed to hesitate as if he wanted to say more, but instead just shrugged and grinned.

I nodded, looking around at the now happy faces of his bullies to the low sound of international soccer piped from the television behind the bar. The owner—he had to be—reached out and pumped my hand when I accepted his offer to shake, enthusiasm as real as his attention.

"You caught me for a fright, little girl," he said with a wink. "But John Fleming's daughter, you be welcome here at The Orange any day of the week. Even during special business hours." He laughed then and his boys laughed with him.

"Nice to hear it," I said, totally thrown by his attitude. "Can I say hello to Dad for you?"

"Malcolm Murray," he said, green eyes glinting, grin tightening to almost feral. "You tell him I took good care of his wee lass, won't you?"

So things weren't as friendly between him and my father as he said. Okay then, I could work with that. "I'll make sure he knows." Whatever dealings Dad had with this man during his days as sheriff, it was pretty clear Malcolm still thought of my father as someone he needed to keep on his good side.

That made me wonder what kind of agreement he'd made with a man who'd clearly found the laws of our town and country to be flexible and not applicable to him. That didn't sound like Dad at all, quite honestly. But I was grateful, at least, he wouldn't find my head in a box on his front step or anything. Discovering my remains would really upset Mom.

"Fetch Miss Fleming a drink," Malcolm said, gesturing to one of his boys. I waved off the offer and smiled, hoping it was an endearing expression despite my lingering nervousness.

"Thanks," I said. "But I'm obviously in the wrong place at the wrong time. I should just be going." I made no attempt to rise, waiting for permission while Malcolm's face fell a little.

"You're here for a reason," he said. "Maybe I can help?"

I never expected that response. "The man I followed here. Simon Jacob." I glanced toward the door where the game was on despite my intrusion. I guess Malcolm would have dealt with me if he needed to. Gulp.

Malcolm nodded once and snapped his fingers. Moments later one of the lumbering bullies returned from the game room with Simon in tow. The flower shop owner looked terrified and began stammering, ignoring me completely, before he even reached the table.

"I have the money, I swear." And that answered the second part of what Simon was into. Drugs and gambling, though that much had been obvious to me when I spotted him at the poker table. Still, confirmation he owed Malcolm didn't hurt. "Pete promised he'd pay."

"Mr. Wilkins has met an untimely demise," Malcolm said, soft and lilting. I really did like his accent, even if he intimidated the hell out of me.

Wait, the way he said it. Did the Irishman have anything to do with…?

Simon began to shake, tears in his eyes. "I'll find the money, Mr. Murray. I swear." So his story flipped with Pete's death. Funny how easily his lie came out. Personally, if Malcolm asked me anything the last thing I'd try to do is deceive him. He seemed the kind of person who could dig out the truth with the right motivation, and money was a powerful motivator.

Simon's deep brown gaze flickered to me as if he only then realized I was there and his dark skin paled to ashen. "Don't tell Terri," he whispered.

None of my business. "Tell me about the arrangement you had with Pete Wilkins." I was feeling a bit more confident, Malcolm watching the exchange like this was the most fun he'd had all week.

Simon shrugged. "I knew it wasn't Dad's signature on those papers," he said. "But Pete heard about my problem." He swallowed, looked to Malcolm who grinned at him like he'd be good to eat with some ketchup and a solid deep frying. "So Pete agreed to pay my debt if I'd keep my mouth shut about the fraud. And I'd pay him back from the funds from the store."

"So you ran the store for him." I wondered if that was Pete's plan for me, too. Find something to hold over my head and profit from Petunia's while I owed him my soul. But what could he blackmail me with? I had nothing he could use against me.

"Terri has no idea." Tears spilled down his dark cheeks.

"About your drug problem either?" I couldn't help but throw that in there. "Did you kill Pete because of it, Simon?"

He flinched then, shook his head. "I swear, I had nothing to do with that. I was here the night Pete died." He sagged in the bully's grasp. "I lost ten grand by 2AM."

Malcolm nodded to me. "Confirmed," he said.

Damn it. Well, at least I knew more about Pete's scam.

"So, you're telling me that piece of garbage Wilkins was taking advantage of good folks. Like the lovely Mistress Iris?" Malcolm's expression darkened, the mood in the bar shifting all over again. His boys certainly took his emotional state personally.

Simon nodded again. "I had no reason to kill him. But now, when Jared finds the paperwork and uncovers what happened, if he decides to take me to court I'll lose the shop for sure." He shuddered. "Owing you and a lawyer would bankrupt me." I had a feeling bankruptcy was the least of Simon's problems, but whatever. His eyes darted left and right and, like a lightbulb coming on, he tried a wavering smile, suddenly eager to please. "That's not all Pete was into. Ask Pitch."

Malcolm's dark expression deepened. "That little shank," he snarled. "Is he hanging out in my alley again?" Another finger snap and tall, dark and bulky #3 or #4—I was losing track of their giant suited bodies—stomped off to the back door. "He's part of Wilkins's little scam?"

"He can tell you everything," Simon said. "I'm sorry, Mr. Murray. I'll find a way to pay you—"

"I know you will. Now shut it." Bully boy had returned, this time with Pitch in his grip. I was surprised the kid had come back, and yet it was his alley, so once I'd gone I guess he didn't think he needed to make himself scarce any longer. Seemed dumb to me though to hang out at a place like The Orange. Unless Malcolm was taking a cut. Not from the furious contempt he aimed at the young man who fought his captor, twisting and snarling in his grasp. Something neither Simon or I had the courage to do. "You, trash," Malcolm snarled. "You selling scripts outside my door again? After the boys told you ever so nicely not to?"

I doubted nice had anything to do with it. And that gambling was okay but drugs weren't.

Pitch shrugged, grinned like this was funny. "Maybe," he said. "Maybe not." His gaze flickered over me, over Simon.

Malcolm stood in a fluid motion, eased toward the young man while my heart caught in my throat. He didn't threaten him with a weapon, just his presence, shorter and much leaner than his men but, from the way he carried himself, far more deadly. My anxiety rose for Pitch as Malcolm stopped before him and patted the plain t-shirt that hugged the young man's narrow chest.

"You smart off with me," the Irishman said in a low tone, "and it'll be the last time. What's your deal with Pete Wilkins then?"

Pitch must have sensed he was in very hot water because his arrogant late teen attitude shifted to nervousness. "He hooked me up with a sweet supplier, selling prescriptions from the nursing home."

I sighed over that. "Alicia?" The young nurse he'd talked to yesterday, she had to be his source.

But Pitch surprised me with a quick headshake. "Not her," he said. "Ruth."

CHAPTER TWENTY-EIGHT

WELL NOW, THAT CERTAINLY added layers to the whole thing, didn't it? Made sense in a lot of ways. I pondered the brother/sister connection while Malcolm spoke again.

"I don't like drugs, boyo," he said. "Don't like them in my establishment or near me in any way." He nodded to me. "Promised your dad years ago, Fee. A bit of sideline distilling, some gambling. No leg breaking or anything like that. Just some friendly business. But drugs." He turned back to Pitch. "You find a new line of employ, you hear? Or a fresh place to do your dirty work."

Pitch sagged and exhaled like he'd been expecting worse. "You're not going to kill me?" The last two words squeaked while my heart thudded at the implications.

Malcolm laughed. Threw his head back, fists on hips and guffawed. Before silencing his humor with an abruptness that made my skin tingle with goosebumps in the sudden silence, broken by the distant cheer of the soccer match TV crowd.

"Not in front of the lady," he said. "Now scoot."

Pitch was half-carried, half-led to the door. I let him go, wanting to talk further with him but not ready to stand up yet. Because I wasn't sure my knees were stable enough to hold me and I didn't want to show weakness.

Malcolm returned to his seat, chuckling. "I have to thank you for a highly entertaining afternoon, lass." He sipped his beer, green eyes sparkling. "You come around any time you want to stir the pot and I'll be your willing audience."

I grinned shakily back. "My pleasure."

"Can my boys escort you home?" That was as clear a command to leave as ever I'd heard one, no matter the kindly way it was delivered. I stood, shaking my head, amazed my legs didn't wobble me right to the floor.

"I'm fine, thank you." I paused and smiled for real. "Thanks for the help."

"Happy to be of service." He tipped his beer bottle to me. "You remember who your friends are in this town, Fee. And don't forget to say hullo to your da for me."

Surreal, standing on the street outside The Orange with my chest heaving for fresh air and that whole encounter behind me. I set off at a trembling walk that evolved into a jog and then a full out sprint all the way to the center of town. I managed to pull myself under control two blocks from home and had even mostly caught my breath by the time I climbed the stairs to Petunia's, hysterical laughter lingering in the back of my throat.

One thing was certain. Dad was on the right track with an investigation into Pete, and maybe I could crack open a new way into the man's fraud with a path my father hadn't considered. I could turn around right now, stop at the sheriff's office, speak to Crew about what just happened. Or go to my parent's house and talk to Dad. Try to. Or, I could find a way to uncover real evidence outside hearsay and the word of a drug dealer and a gambling addict. Like the paperwork I knew now hid in the construction trailer at the new equestrian center site.

But was I really up for breaking and entering? Knowing doing so could ruin any case against Pete Wilkins, dead or not? I hesitated with my hand on the front door knob. Blackmail. What if the information Pete had wasn't about me, but about my father? That would be reason to kill him.

And that meant B&E was in my cards after all. Because whatever it was Pete Wilkins was using to silence my father, I was going to find it before the state troopers did.

I was happy to send Daisy home, to see the backsides of the grumpy Jones duo, to tuck in my guests and go downstairs to my apartment. To dress all in black while Petunia watched with huge eyes as if sensing what I was about to do. I couldn't ask anyone to come watch over the B&B, not without cancelling out my alibi. I'd just have to trust that the quiet house over my head would remain that way and that, after midnight, I was safe enough to sneak out and go looking for the evidence I was now afraid pinned Pete's death on my father.

Was it a good thing I managed to escape Petunia's without anyone seeing me? Should I have been alarmed at how clean my getaway, how obviously talented I was at sneaking about? Regardless, with my phone on silent but forwarded from the B&B just in case there was an emergency—the best I could do under the circumstances—I backed my car out of the driveway by taking it out of gear and let it drift down the hill a few seconds before staring the engine and chugging for the edge of town.

I had no idea if construction was at a standstill while Pete's death was sorted out, but at least the site was dark when I arrived, my headlights out but the parking ones giving me enough illumination to coast to a stop on the far side of the long, narrow trailer that served as the office. A work truck stood silent and dark on the far end of the lot, but the lack of movement or any kind of activity told me it had to be one left overnight. Only the sound of crickets and a breeze ruffling nearby pine trees disturbed the night, an owl hooting its disapproval at me when I climbed the metal steps and tried the door, just in case.

And found it open. Shocked by this turn of events, I slipped inside, delighted at my luck, and looked around. Dark, so dark, but my eyes adjusted enough I made out a desk at one end and a line of filing cabinets at the other. My target.

The small flashlight on my keychain gave me the clarity I needed to sort through the drawers, most of it relating to Pete's business dealings. I think it was more luck than skill that I stumbled on a file marked, "Reading and Weep" that paused my fingers and made me whistle. Sounded like the kind of sick sense of humor that Pete Wilkins might use to celebrate his fraud against land owners. And, when I flipped it open to look inside, there was the paperwork for Petunia's right on top, staring me in the face. Grandmother Iris's faked signature front and center. I quickly compared the one from the letter I'd taken from the house, confirming to myself even after a stroke there was no way this one Pete tried to pass off could be anything but forged. I'd seen my grandmother's post stroke writing, all wobbly and disjointed. And it looked nothing like the signature on the deed papers.

Pete tried to bamboozle me. And as long as Crew was willing to let me use the letter she left behind in the nursing home as evidence, I now had proof Petunia's was completely and utterly mine.

I didn't have time to celebrate. Not when the door to the office opened and light flooded it as someone flicked the switch. I looked up, shocked and utterly caught in the act, to find Jared Wilkins staring back at me.

CHAPTER TWENTY-NINE

NEITHER OF US SPOKE for a long moment, Jared standing in the open doorway, me holding the file containing the evidence I needed against his father. The truck on the lot. Not a regular overnight, then. Probably Jared's, parked there while he took a look around? Whatever the case, he was obviously the reason the door to the office was unlocked when I got here. Stupid, Fee. Just stupid.

When he finally did break our stillness, it was to come further into the trailer, letting the door swing shut with an eerie creaking behind him.

"Tell me why I shouldn't call the sheriff right now." He sounded tired more than angry, and looked it, face pale and drawn. He had his mother's eyes, not the beady, watchful ones I remembered from his dad on our single encounter. Less intimidating and more human even now in this most wretched of situations. So I took a chance Daisy was right about him and offered up the file.

Jared crossed to me, took the paperwork, looked down. Rifled through the pages. Looked up again as I spoke.

"Your father and aunt have a lot to answer for," I said. "I'm hoping you weren't part of it."

Jared left me there, turning to cross to the desk, taking a seat as he sorted through the papers. Making no effort to call Crew. He offered me the ones at the top holding them up with an eyebrow cocked and I joined him, tentatively trusting I made the right choice, perching on a thin metal stool while my shaking hands grasped the pages and made them rattle.

"Looks like Dad had something against you," Jared said in that same dull tone.

I frowned instantly, rejecting such an idea, looked down. And found a printout of a bank account with a lot of money in it, like hundreds of thousands. With my name on it. At the branch of the bank where

Ryan and I used to do business in New York. Presumably where he still did.

What the hell?

"This isn't mine." I shook my head, struggling with the contents.

"Wouldn't have mattered to my father," Jared said. "As long as he had something he could blackmail you with."

"So you knew about the scheme?" I didn't want to believe it, not when Jared's phone remained in his pocket and he made no move yet to have me arrested. Surely Daisy pegged him as the good guy he really was? How could I possibly reconcile that with a man who would stand by while his father ruined people?

"No," Jared said. "But I suspected. And I think I might have given him the means to do it." He leaned back in the chair, the faint squeaking making me nervous. "My specialty is IT." He gestured at the pile of papers. "Dad had me investigating people, but I didn't find out until later they weren't investors he wanted backgrounds on but folks he was planning to steal from."

I sagged on the stool, feeling terrible for him, wishing I had comfort to share. While my mind uncoiled and realized who had opened this bank account in my name. "Ryan," I snarled. "My ex. He set me up. He doesn't have this kind of money. He has to be embezzling. And is making it look like I'm part of it." Cheating was one thing, but now? Now the man was dead. Murder wasn't beyond me, it turned out.

Jared sat forward. "Looks that way," he said. "But I'm happy to chase down the cash trail for you, if that helps. If we can find where it came from—and had nothing to do with you—we can turn the cops on to him and you'll be in the clear."

I gaped at him before managing to speak. "Why would you help me?" Especially after I broke into his property and found evidence against his father.

"Because I'm not Pete Wilkins." Jared sounded angry suddenly, face set, jaw jumping, eyes locked on the file before him. "And I never will be." Jared's hands tightened into fists on the desk before him. "I've been such a fool all these years. Trusting him. Believing him. But when I found out what he was up to…"

The fight Daisy witnessed. "You confronted him."

Jared nodded, slow and sad. "I didn't kill him, Fiona. I swear it. But, as horrible as it sounds, I'm not upset he's dead." He flinched, met my eyes like I'd judge him for that.

I reached forward, squeezed his wrist until his hands unclenched. "Thank you for being a good person, Jared. We'll figure this out." I hesitated. "You do have an alibi?" He jerked a bit as if to protest but I shook my head. "The sheriff told me last night the state troopers are getting involved. I thought you should know."

Jared exhaled. "I do," he said.

"Your mother?" But he hesitated before shaking his head. "Does she have one, too?"

Jared looked away. "That's her story to tell," he said.

I sat back, staring sightlessly at Ryan's betrayal. "And the drug thefts from the nursing home?" That really got Jared's attention. He hissed and stared in shock. "So you didn't know?"

One last head shake, Jared's voice muted by visible surprise.

"I think it's the little nurse, the blonde. You know the one I mean. I saw her leaving your house the other day." His face shifted even as I spoke, from surprise to denial.

"Not Alicia," he said. Then went silent, guilty.

"Your alibi, I take it," I said. How interesting. Did Pete know his son was dating the young woman he forced into skimpy suits and obviously had a thing for?

Jared sighed, shrugged. "I guess it doesn't matter now. Here." He fished papers out of a drawer and handed them to me, more bank information. But these had his name on them. "You want embezzled funds, a page from your old boyfriend's book. An account in my name. Dad was so unoriginal. But he was setting me up, just like your ex was doing to you. Except I think Dad was actually trying to make me look guilty while your boyfriend was just covering his ass in case the authorities came calling."

Not much better, in my estimation, but a fraction less evil, I guess. "How many people has he stolen property from?"

"I don't know the full numbers," Jared said, "not yet. But it's in the dozens if not more. Mostly out of towners with aging family here in Reading and no one to take over power of attorney. Or care enough to visit." He sounded saddened by that and, frankly, so was I when I thought about it. I'd left home, run off first to college then the big city, hadn't visited outside a day or two here and there in ten years. Would I have been that person who let my father or mother languish in the Reading Nursing Care facility without love or support until they died and Pete took their property? The thought of someone like him claiming Mom and Dad's house made me want to scream.

And think about the big question I'd been pondering. "Why would he suddenly start bilking locals? Surely he had to know that made him vulnerable?" I set the pages aside, no longer wanting to touch the evidence of Ryan's duplicity or Pete's acts against his son.

"I don't know," Jared said. "It doesn't make sense. I don't think Dad was the one getting the signatures, or forging the few he couldn't wrangle."

"Ruth again?" It connected.

But Jared seemed hesitant. "Maybe. But my aunt is about as friendly and kind as a crocodile, which means she'd have trouble getting anyone to trust her."

True enough. "We need to get this evidence to Crew," I said.

Jared gathered the paperwork, tucked it back into the file and handed it to me, eyes clear and lips in a grim line. "That's why I was here," he said. "I came tonight to look for evidence, hoping I wouldn't find anything. And the very first papers I stumble on targeted me. His own son." Jared cleared his throat, voice thick. "I went out for air, heard you pull up, watched you come inside." Yeah, I was so good at sneaking around. Master breaker and enterer, that's me. "I didn't know what to do. But in the end, there wasn't anything else I *could* do." Jared's expression calmed, resignation winning. "I need this over with. For me. For Mom. To get him out of our lives forever." Jared paused before his face relaxed further, a faint smile there. "Thank you, Fee."

I didn't know what to say to that. "I didn't kill him," I said.

Jared laughed. "I didn't think you did. Whatever the reason Dad was at your place that night, snooping around his new acquisition, I can't imagine you did him in. If anything he really did slip and fall and hit his head and drown. Because karma is a bitch, isn't she?"

I stood, headed for the door. Wanted to ask him more about Alicia, but figured I'd let him have his privacy about her. I could track her down and grill her personally. As for his mother…

"If you hated him so much," I said, "why didn't you two leave him?"

"Isn't it obvious?" Jared sounded bitter, smile gone, eyes locked on the desk, hands in fists on either side of the blotter. "He was blackmailing my mother. And I wouldn't abandon her to him, Fee. Not for anything."

Which meant Aundrea made it to the top of my suspect list all over again.

CHAPTER THIRTY

I SHOULD HAVE GONE right to Crew. Or Dad. Instead, about twenty minutes later, I sat in a different kind of hot water, the best kind, with my chin in bubbles and the B&B none the worse for wear for my absence, mind spinning.

The two places I did my best thinking? Running and in the tub. But honestly, I just needed a little pampering right now. I'd escaped a possibly terrible fate thanks to Jared's kindness and understanding. And thanks to the file sitting on my dresser, hopefully everything with Petunia's would get sorted out in short order. But I had suspects to consider and wasn't all that hopeful Crew wouldn't look at my dad even more carefully considering the new evidence against me generated by that piece of crap I used to live with. Or turn his attention back on me, for that matter, though the only one really at risk of imminent death at this point was Ryan. The creep.

"He'll pay, Petunia," I said to the pug who stared at me from the edge of the tub, big eyes bracketed by perked black ears. "After I skin him alive."

She grunted in agreement.

"Aundrea makes the most sense at this point, unless she has an alibi. Though Jared seemed reluctant to say anything which makes me wonder if he's protecting her from something." Son protecting mother like me protecting Dad? Made me feel like Jared and I had a lot more in common than I first thought. "It's pretty clear she hated her husband and why. At least, in the general sense. If Pete was blackmailing his own wife to keep her…" Just gross.

Petunia whined softly at me before heaving herself up, front paws on the tile surround of the tub. I patted her head briefly, a fluff of suds on her cheek, before rambling on.

"I have to go through that evidence more carefully before I hand it over." That had been my excuse for keeping it to myself as I drove home. "To make sure there really isn't anything that can incriminate Dad."

Petunia clearly didn't think much of my plan. Or, had her own ideas about what to do next. Because she chose that moment to lurch forward with a mighty effort and landed in my lap. Water and bubbles flew everywhere while I squealed in shocked protest, the pug grinning at me in her doggy way before swiping my wet face with her tongue.

"Fine," I snarled. "I'll take the file to Crew. Happy?"

From her huffing delight, she was.

Of course, I wasn't going to go beating on his door at one in the morning. Instead, I tucked into bed, mind still whirling, the pug attempting three times to join me before she sadly curled up on the floor with an accusatory stare that was hard to ignore.

Dawn came without a wink of sleep. By the time I finally decided I wasn't going to manage any rest in my present state of mind, dressed and made it upstairs, I had poured myself coffee set to perk the night before only to stop in shock and stare around the silent kitchen.

Two seconds before Mary and Betty, their grumpy expressions matching, walked through the swinging door.

I don't know who was more surprised, me or them. The fact I'd finally—finally!—beat them to the punch should have given me a sense of accomplishment. Instead, I sighed and leaned a hip against the counter, saluting them with my mug.

"Morning, ladies," I said. "Busy day ahead."

Mary muttered agreement, not a hint of her normally sullen state in evidence. She actually looked impressed. Betty scuttled to the stove to begin breakfast while I headed for the foyer to check my schedule. Maybe this was a good sign? Though if I had to not sleep to be the first one at the helm of Petunia's I was going to have a very unhappy life.

I set my mug next to the ledger and turned on the computer on the sidebar, checking my bookings while Petunia wandered from the kitchen to sit on my sandaled feet. Mary had given her breakfast, from the way the pug licked her chops, and when she stared up at me with that accusing expression I finally growled at her.

"Can I please sort out my day first before I possibly incriminate myself in Pete Wilkins's murder and embezzling money from Ryan's law firm? Thank you."

Petunia grunted at me before farting her opinion of that particular procrastination.

The front door opened, saving me from further discussion with the pug who woofed a short greeting when Peggy entered. Cookie wiggled in her arms, a sweet little orange bow her adornment for the day, while the old lady balanced a shoe box in one arm and the happy little dog in the other.

I hurried to her, divested her of the package with a soft pat for Cookie while my neighbor beamed her delight.

"I promised you Iris's things," she said. "And I know you're busy, so we'll do tea another time. But I wanted you to have these." She smiled down at the box with moisture rimming her faded eyes. "Iris would have loved that."

"Thank you so much, Peggy," I said, carrying the box to the sidebar and opening it. The box itself was old, maybe from the seventies from the faded print and the dust on the lid. I picked through a few photos, one of Peggy herself and Grandmother Iris, the two seated on a sofa with a big old clock behind them. I teared up at the sight, my grandmother looking far older than I'd ever remembered her.

"Dear Iris," Peggy said, wiping at one cheek while Cookie wriggled and licked her fingers. "I miss her so." She met my eyes. "Any luck finding out who killed that terrible man who tried to take Petunia's from you?"

She was such a dear. "Not yet," I said, wrinkling my nose. No need for her to think I was putting myself in trouble. "Crew is taking care of everything."

Peggy's face lit up and she patted my cheek. "That's wonderful to hear, dear," she said. "I just know it will all get sorted out and you'll be back to normal in no time."

I hugged her on impulse, feeling her slim body shake against me with a palsy tremor, thin bones so fragile while her sweet little dog snuggled against my arm. "I really appreciate the delivery," I said. "I promise I'll make time for tea." It was the least I could do.

Peggy left, waving and blinking through a smile while I turned back to the box. So many bits and pieces, including a twin to the butterfly hair pin I had found in her things from the nursing home, the first now safely tucked in my jewelry box downstairs. Some papers, faded ticket stubs and evidence of Grandmother Iris's friendship with Peggy.

I didn't get to finish going through the contents, my moment of sad reminiscence about my grandmother cut short as once again the front door opened. But this visitor wasn't welcome, not by a long shot.

Vivian didn't seem to care I scowled at her intrusion, her pristine jogging suit in pale blue velvet screaming girl of privilege, step aside, peasant. Her joggers looked like she hadn't had them on her feet ever and the pert ponytail she sported looked so teased and contrived if she ever sweated in it she'd be a disaster in about two seconds.

She came right to me, leaning over the small podium I used as a front desk, bright eyes sharp and full of delight. Which could only mean bad things for me.

"I know your secret," she hissed. "And I have no compunction about turning you in."

"What the hell is that supposed to mean?" What exactly did she think she had on me? Did Jared tell her about Ryan's embezzling? No, I couldn't bring myself to believe that.

Vivian tossed that ponytail like it was a weapon, holding up her cell phone so I could see the picture she took of me in the side street at The Orange talking to Pitch as I connected the dots. “Stay away from Crew Turner,” she snarled, “or I’m telling him you’re a druggie who buys prescription drugs from teenaged boys in dark alleys.”

CHAPTER THIRTY-ONE

I LAUGHED IN HER face. For quite a while, pretty sure the longer I went at it the more likely it was her head would explode. Which kept me laughing long past the time it was actually funny. If her statement/threat/accusation was ever funny. When I finally sobered, I leaned in too, grinning in her red cheeked face.

"Now that we have that out of the way," I said, "what do you want, Vivian?"

"I saw you." She jabbed her index finger with the sharpened point of her manicure into my chest then at the phone screen. "With that kid who deals outside The Orange. Yesterday."

"Really," I said. Pulled a huge ah-ha out of my ass and presented it to her for her observation. "And how, exactly, would you know someone like Pitch sells drugs outside a place like that if you weren't a customer yourself?" Because logic, people.

She obviously hadn't thought her little blackmail scheme through, much worse at it than Pete Wilkins. Vivian stammered a moment before huffing in my face and leaving without another word. Looking slightly less sure of herself and markedly more anxious about trying to threaten me.

So, she dabbled in the prescription drug trade, did she? User, more than likely. I imagined Crew would be delighted to know that. Speaking of whom, I had a delivery to make and wasn't sure if he was going to toss me in a jail cell or say thank you. Or both.

Time to find out.

Twenty minutes later, Daisy firmly ensconced in the foyer directing traffic, I slipped out the front door, the previously pouting pug on her leash now panting happily as she followed me, for once my pace keeping time with hers, to the sheriff's office. So what if I lingered when Petunia decided to sniff a mailbox or two? Were we in a hurry? Well, considering the file folder in my giant bag was burning a hole through the worn leather—or I imagined it was—I really should have been. Didn't speed my lethargic steps up the stairs to the front entry, or do much to raise my spirits when I spotted Crew talking to Robert and the blonde female deputy on the far side of the gate separating the front from the bullpen.

Did he just roll his eyes at me? Okay then, fine. I whipped out the folder and brandished it with enthusiasm, catching his attention. About thirty seconds later, I stood with Petunia sitting on my feet while Crew Turner thumped the folder on his desk and told me in no uncertain terms what he thought of my continuing participation in his investigation.

"What part of mind your own damned business don't you understand, Fee?" Crew's pulsing forehead vein was back. He really did need to get that checked.

"You're welcome," I shot back, Petunia farting for good measure. Crew scowled down at the dog before shaking his head, running one hand through his hair in clear exasperation.

"What is it about the Fleming family that makes me want to shake the lot of you for being so stubborn?" He ground his teeth together. "No, just two of you."

Before he could speak further and probably kick my ass out of his office, I told him everything in a rush of information he absorbed by sinking, with his face paling and his eyes growing huge, into his chair while I told him not only about Pitch and Simon and the gambling at The Orange but my suspicions about Ruth and Pete and the drug trade.

"Let me get this straight," Crew said ever so softly when I ground to a halt at last, stopping short of admitting I'd broken into Jared's property last night, instead leaving the sheriff with the impression the young Wilkins and I were helping each other. The less he knew the better, and it wasn't like Jared was going to press charges. "You've been stumbling around Reading, interfering with ongoing investigations—shut it for one second, missy, and listen—and you expect me to thank you for bringing this to me?"

Did he just call me *missy*?

"That's right," I said. Loudly and with conviction. "You're freaking welcome for doing your stupid ass job for you, Crew Turner. Because I haven't seen one bit of police work come out of this office since this whole mess started."

"That's right," Crew said, voice low and dangerous as I realized I'd crossed a big line with him. "You haven't. Because I don't advertise what I'm doing, who I'm talking to or what I suspect, Fee. That's not my job. My job is to catch bad guys as quickly and quietly as possible. Unlike you," he thudded one fist down on his desk, making Petunia fart again, "who rolls through town like a wrecking ball ruining my chance at uncovering what's really going on!" He stood abruptly, lunging for me, grasping my upper arm and lifting me from the chair, swinging me around, shoving me toward the closed door he just opened in time to keep me from running right into it. "If I catch you snooping around, I'm arresting you."

"For what?" I pulled on Petunia's leash to make sure he didn't cut her in half when he shoved me the rest of the way out of his office and grasped the door with that same hand.

"I'll think of something!" Slam.

Okay then. Be a dick. See if I cared.

Petunia hummed and grunted and snorted at me all the way back to the B&B but I ignored her, my lower lip gnawed raw by the time we made it home. Was Crew right? Was I getting in the way? But I'd uncovered so much that he didn't even seem to know about. Was that why he was so angry? Had to be. I was ahead of him and his little boy ego couldn't handle it.

That is, or I was actually making things worse for him and myself and my dad all rolled into one.

Daisy took one look at me and held her tongue for once, so I must have appeared premiumly pissed off and primed for an explosion. I took ten minutes down in my apartment to punch my pillow after screaming into it until I saw stars before gulping down a hot cup of coffee and heading back to work.

But no matter what I did, no matter how hard I tried, I just spun down into deeper anger and frustration. Finally, about 2PM, Daisy jerked me aside when I hung up the phone on a cancellation so hard the plastic casing cracked.

"Get out," she said in the sweetest tone of voice ever. "Now. Before you hurt someone. Like me."

I shook my head, slumping. "I'm sorry, Daisy," I said. "I'm just…"

"I know." She shook me a little, faint smile full of compassion. "You're dealing with a lot. Listen, I don't have anything going on tonight. Why don't you get out, go shopping, take a break from all this." Her perky suggestion made me want to hide in my room and watch TV until I was a zombie but I nodded finally and grabbed my purse.

Daisy scooped up Petunia and waved her front paw at me as I disappeared back out into the mean streets of Reading with every intention of doing exactly what Daisy told me to do. But there was only so many touristy crap shops I could visit, so many expensive boutiques I could raise my eyebrows at. Until I finally relented and headed for the one place perhaps I should have avoided after the few days I'd had.

Turned out Dad wasn't home anyway. A quick cup of coffee with Mom gave me that much.

"Gone to the pub," she said with an I don't care air. "You two really need to try to schedule visits instead of popping in on each other like you do."

"Dad's been to the B&B?" I had no idea.

"A few times," Mom shrugged. "So have I. You know, for a business woman trying to run a very busy place like Petunia's, you're not home much."

She didn't use that tone of disappointment, but it was close, so close. Close enough I winced and admitted to myself she was right.

Didn't stop me from hurrying off to The Harp and Thorn to try to catch Dad when I was done with Mom, only to have mostly drunk but clearly able to serve Patrick shake his head at me. No John Fleming in days.

Grunt. Where the hell was he, then?

As luck would have it, when I dragged myself up the drive, half hidden by my car, I caught a glimpse of Dad's truck in my peripheral vision. My intention to go back into Petunia's and do my job despite Daisy's insistence vanished as I leaped behind the wheel and followed him.

Not because I really wanted to talk to him, nope. Because Dad wasn't alone in his truck and the blonde hair of the woman in the passenger seat was a far cry from Mom's dark shade of red.

Either Dad wasn't paying attention or I held enough distance between us he didn't seem to realize I was behind him as he drove out of town. Distracted? By the blonde beside him? They were talking, I could see that much through the back window of his pickup, animatedly, too. The girl's hands were active, her body half turned toward my father as she spoke.

He turned off with lots of warning, and I knew exactly where he was heading before he even hit the blinker. The cabin his father left him had been one of those places I'd had a love/hate relationship with as a kid. Love because it was fun to hang out with my father and fish and track animals through the woods. And hate thanks to the fact he cancelled our trips five times out of six because of work.

I drove past the turn and waited a moment before reversing and following. I kept telling myself I didn't have to hunt him down like this, I could let him know I was here. That Dad had nothing to hide, nothing. And I was overreacting. But there was a horrible, painful moment when I parked my car, got out, tracked through the woods in time to see Dad get out of his truck and help the blonde from the passenger seat.

A blonde I knew immediately. Who followed Dad to the cabin and disappeared inside with him.

Alicia Conway. Oh, Dad.

I have no idea how I got to the door, how long I pounded on it with my fist before it jerked wide and my father, his big face stunned and then closed, stared down at me. I wanted to punch him as I had the door, to beat on him and scream at him. For cheating on Mom. With a floozy girl who worked for Pete Wilkins.

Wait a second.

Dad exhaled, sagged, stepped aside. "You might as well come in," he said. "It's time I told you everything."

Alicia stood from the rickety wooden bench that bracketed the kitchen table, flushing dark red but not out of guilt. From fear. Her eyes flickered to Dad who waved off her anxiety.

"It's okay," he said. "Tell Fee what you're doing here."

"Helping John build a case against Pete," she said. And started to cry.

CHAPTER THIRTY-TWO

I GLARED UP AT Dad who hurried forward, suddenly soft and kind, something I'd never seen from him. He hugged her gently, giant form towering over her, and she clung to him like he was her lifeline.

What the actual hell and who was this man? Because he was not my father.

"Alicia's been working with me for months," Dad said over her sniffling. "Since Pete hired her to be his assistant."

"Did you tell Dad about the drugs?" I glared at Alicia, accusing her while not really knowing for sure if she was connected.

Dad flinched, looked down at her with a frown. "Drugs?"

Alicia sobbed again, sinking onto the bench, face in her hands. "It wasn't me," she wailed. "It was Pitch."

My father looked like she'd gut punched him. "Alicia. If you've done anything to jeopardize the case—"

"Dad." I hit him with that word. Caught his attention. "There is no case. Pete Wilkins is dead."

Alicia gulped while Dad tried to find words to refute me.

"Pitch is my brother," she whispered to me. "He thought I could help him make a few extra bucks, to get him out of trouble. Convinced me no one would miss the prescriptions."

Dad paled and joined her on the bench. I sat across from them, waited.

"But Ruth found out," she hiccupped past her tears. "I thought I'd be fired. Instead, she funneled even more drugs through me to Pitch, blackmailing me into being her mule. Sent me out of town with Pete on regular trips to deliver goods to other dealers." Alicia turned to Dad with giant eyes and more tears, one slim hand landing on his forearm, vulnerable and weak. "Please, John, I'm sorry. I should have told you. But I was afraid and the drugs had nothing to do with Pete's fraud around his building sites or the deed signatures."

"Did Pete have anything to do with the drugs?" Dad's normally stern tone and expression were back. Well that was more like it and I didn't have the creeps anymore.

Alicia shook her head. "That was all Ruth," she said. "I'm pretty sure if Pete found out he'd be furious with her. Too risky." No wonder the poor kid was a wreck. Ruth on one side thanks to her brother, Pete on the other, gross. And Dad bullying her into turning evidence. Wow, she was a lot tougher than I had given her credit for.

"How did you end up Pete's assistant then?" If Ruth had a good thing going, why end it?

"She didn't trust his side of the other business," she said. "The fraud and building code violations. The thefts of construction materials. And the property acquisitions." She shrugged. "While the trips gave me the chance to get the drugs out of state."

"So she sent you to be her eyes and ears as well as her mule." That made sense. "Why did you turn on him?"

"Jared." Alicia finally smiled, hand falling from Dad's arm. He rubbed at the spot where her fingers had been, a faint flash of guilt on his face as he caught my eyes. Boys and their hormones. Mom would kick his butt for being such an idiot about a pretty girl. "I met him and… he's amazing. Nothing like Pete. I've been telling John that." She seemed keen we both believe her and since I'd had my own dealings with the younger Wilkins, I just nodded for her to go on. "I fell in love with him, and he with me. I'd do anything to help him and this is my only way to do that." So she was his alibi for sure then. "I was with Jared the night Pete died." She flushed. "All night."

Well, good for them.

"Okay, Dad," I said, fixing him with a hard glare. "Your turn. You weren't fishing with the guys." He looked away, swallowed as I went on. "Where were you the night Pete died?"

My father sighed then, elbows on the table, glancing at Alicia. "Out of state," he said like it hurt him. "Talking to a connection of Pete's about the construction fraud."

"Despite the fact the case was dropped officially," I said, "and you are no longer sheriff and have no jurisdiction to investigate further."

Dad bobbed a nod. And I laughed. That made him flinch then grunt, then grin.

"Poor Crew," I said, snickering. "No wonder he's pissed at us."

Dad's white teeth flashed, wolf like. "Maybe if that boy would use the sense God gave him," he said. Exhaled deeply. "I've been gathering further evidence against Pete, to ensure those who were victimized get justice."

"Even after he died." I nodded. "That's my dad."

Giant relief flooded me, made me a bit giddy. So my father was innocent. That left Aundrea and Ruth Wilkins. "You need to tell Crew where you were, Dad. The state troopers are coming and he'll be handing over evidence that could point at you."

Dad shrugged that off like it didn't matter. "I can present what I need to prove my alibi if I have to," he said. Paused, gave me the stink eye. "Can you?"

That made me laugh again, though with a little less delight. "So we've been suspecting each other all along then, have we?"

Dad didn't say anything. But Alicia did.

"I told him you didn't," she whispered. "It had to be Ruth."

"Or Aundrea?" Why not Pete's wife?

Alicia hesitated. "I don't know about that," she said, clearly lying.

I let it go for the moment, told them both about the papers I'd found with Jared, handed over to Crew. Dad took a second to be pissed at me for not bringing them to him before shrugging.

"What would you do with it, Dad? You're not sheriff anymore."

That wasn't fair and I regretted the words the second they left my mouth despite the fact they were true. He seemed to deflate, losing his power while Alicia stared back and forth between us with her mouth gaping.

"You're right, Fee," he said, sad and low. "But I really wanted to see this through. I didn't want this one case hanging over me, you know?"

I nodded, regret pushing me forward to squeeze his big hand. He squeezed back, smiled a little.

"Chip off the old blockhead," he said. "I should never have kept you from law enforcement."

Now he told me.

"Dad," I said, tears stinging the corners of my eyes, "you're my hero, no matter what."

He blinked, I blinked and we shared a moment. The first one in a long, long time. Wait, ever. Until Alicia cleared her throat and broke it wide open again, stirring the need to snarl at her which I suppressed just in time.

"What are we going to do?" She again looked at both of us, back and forth, like I might have a plan she hadn't considered.

"Nothing." Dad set both big hands on the table, palms flat, face set. "We're done. All of us." He glared at me. "Crew has what he needs, if you're right about what you handed over. As for Ruth, Alicia's willing to turn her in for protection. So we'll see what our new sheriff says about confidential informants and immunity for her and Pitch."

He didn't sound hopeful.

CHAPTER THIRTY-THREE

I LEANED IN TO Dad when Alicia excused herself to use the washroom, watching her go as I spoke.

"You're a big idiot," I said. "Why didn't you just tell me?"

"Same," he said. And sighed. "Never mind," he winked at me, good humor in his eyes, "you tried to, didn't you? So, I'll accept the idiot label. If you'll admit you thought your old man killed Pete Wilkins." He seemed highly amused by that.

"Not as bad as you thinking your daughter did," I said. Paused. "Or the fact you used to associate with Malcolm Murray."

Dad flinched, paled. "What are you talking about?"

I told him about how I'd followed Simon, the encounter with the old Irishman. I'd seen my dad a lot of things, but never truly afraid. Not until that moment when he grasped my hand, smothering my little one in his big grip, tight and shaking.

"Promise me," he said, "you'll stay away from Malcolm Murray."

Alicia returned before I could respond though I'm sure from the startled look I knew crossed my face my father figured out I was about as nervous of The Orange's owner as he was. Not like I was thinking about hanging out there or anything. But it was clear my father wasn't done keeping secrets.

We all got up to leave, Alicia begging off because of a headache. I followed her, Dad striding ahead to the truck, but she paused at the door and bumped into me. I was so surprised by her sudden turn, I stared into her eyes, felt the cold press of metal in my hand before I could react.

"Be careful if you're going to do what I think you're going to do," she whispered. "She's ruthless. No pun intended."

She spun then and hurried to Dad, leaving me to watch them go, to look down after they had at the small key in my hand, etched on one side with the word *Office*. It looked old enough to be for the main door of the administration area of the nursing home I knew exactly what Alicia was insinuating. And though I'd considered just stopping and walking away, how could I now? Now that I had the means to break into the head nurse/administrator's office and get the evidence Crew needed to put her away?

No. I needed to give it to Dad, to the new sheriff. Or the state troopers coming as early as tomorrow. Not sneak off for another breaking and entering session. I highly doubted Ruth would be as kind or understanding as Jared had been.

Putting civic duty ahead of my own burning need to see this through, I headed instead to the sheriff's office, my curiosity held in very tight control. Only to find Crew gone for the day and a grinning Robert behind the front desk.

"Fanny," my hateful cousin said with a leering grin that did nothing to endear him to me. "Here with more evidence?" He snorted a laugh, glancing into the bullpen where one of the other deputies—

the woman who had collected evidence—rolled her eyes at me and went back to her work.

"Crew's not here?" His office door stood open.

"Nope, gone," Robert said, leaning back to prop his feet up on the desk, arms crossing behind his head. "I can take care of whatever it is you think might be important enough for the sheriff."

Like I'd trust him with a blessed thing. "Forget it," I said. "I'll call him tomorrow."

Frustration drove me out the door, down the steps, to the sound of Robert calling after me.

"See ya, Fanny!"

I really, really, really hated that nickname. Stood on the sidewalk, staring down at the key in my hand, hating Robert, furious with Dad for chasing me away from what I really loved, if I'd just admit it to myself—law enforcement. And made a terrible, terrible decision.

The nursing home was the final piece that could prove who killed Pete, I was sure of it. If Alicia was right and Ruth murdered her own brother, there would be a reason for it. And him finding out his horrid sister was selling drugs out of the home would be a massive one. Imagine him trying to blackmail his own sibling? She was scary just from our initial contact and the way Alicia talked about her, well. I could wrap this case up tonight.

Alicia gave me the key, so she trusted me. Maybe she even knew what I was thinking, that Ruth's guilt could be proven by a visit to her office. Yes, that had to be it, didn't it? Alicia gave me the means to end this. But why not give it to Dad?

Because he was too focused on Pete. Ah, the lies we tell ourselves when we want to be right. One thing I did know, if Ruth found out the state troopers were coming—small town, word had to be getting around—surely she would make sure to dump whatever evidence might incriminate her on the drug thefts. Let alone Pete's murder. That was it, decision made. My car hiccupped its distress at my choice but I ignored it in favor of courage fed by the need to act.

My father's daughter indeed.

Night was falling by the time I pulled into the driveway, the blue light of dusk casting the last shadows that faded into darkness while I approached the front door of the nursing home like I owned the place and swept inside. I wondered then if this was what Daisy had in mind for my night off and fought a hysterical giggle at the thought. The office door was closed, no light shining within, the foyer empty of all but the soft sounds of horribly recreated pop music on the crackling, tinny speakers.

There were bound to be security cameras, but I couldn't worry about that now. The office door gave way under my hand, unlocking smoothly with the key. That made me nervous as I stepped inside and closed the door, breathing a little too heavily. How could I get into Ruth's inner sanctum if this key was for the main door?

I needn't have worried. When I reached the door knob to her personal space, tucking in next to the tall filing cabinet and pile of boxes that were the last remaining possessions of the deceased, the key did its job all over again. I snorted to myself at her lack of originality and cheapskate ways. Two locks, one key. Honestly.

Muffled voices penetrated the wall to my right, the sound of arguing, low but discernable. One voice was deep, graveled, had to be Ruth. The other? Female, yes. Otherwise I had no idea. But now nervousness really kicked in. What was I thinking? Standing in the darkness of the administrator's office looking for what exactly?

And then, like fate was finally on my side, I saw it. Eyes adjusting to the darkness, the big, metal door half open. The safe gaping and waiting for me.

That meant Ruth was only gone a moment, had likely been distracted and left to deal with whoever it was she talked to. As long as I heard their voices through the thin walls, I had time. My trusty penlight dangled from my keychain, lighting up the inside of the old fashioned iron safe, filled with paper files and a large plastic envelope I peeked into.

Pills. A lot of pills in different colors, all sealed into zip lock bags. Ready for Pitch to pick up and distribute or Alicia to carry off out of state? A quick glance at the file at the top of the pile gave me a purchase order, with a second file beneath it doubling that order. Two sets of paperwork, and one giant scam.

Gotcha.

My phone on camera, I snapped as many pictures as I could with my hands trembling in eager excitement. The low light and pinpoint of the flash worried me a bit about focus, but this was the best I could do without outright stealing the files and I was sure if Ruth found them missing she'd either disappear too or find a way to dispute the evidence.

Like how it was illegally obtained by the owner of a B&B where her dead brother's drowned body was found?

Yeah, like that.

The voices moved, getting louder. Panic struck as I spun toward the office door. Caught a glimpse through the glass of Ruth's back, and Aundrea Wilkins, red faced and shaking, saying something low and threatening. Trapped and with discovery imminent, I did the only thing I could think of.

With a faint squeak of fear, Ruth's voice echoing, "That's that last I want to hear about this, Aundrea," heralding her approach about as much as the squelching of her giant sneakers, I tucked under her desk with my arms around my knees and hoped I hadn't just signed my own death warrant trying to be a hero.

The main office door closed with a bang, followed by the slam of Ruth's. Yeah, I was doomed.

CHAPTER THIRTY-FOUR

TIME SLOWED TO A crawl, my heartbeat thudding in my ears, entire body shaking while the squish-squish-squish sound of Ruth's sneakers drew closer. Any second now she'd pass the edge of her desk, close her safe, turn and—

And find me hiding in the worst possible place an idiot like me could hide in a (suspected) murderer's office. I clasped one hand over my mouth to keep from screaming as the first white toed foot appeared, the hem of her lab coat, big calf lined with varicose veins thicker than a pencil. Fascination and terror mingled as the scent of disinfectant traveled with her in a waft so powerful I choked on it.

I was so dead.

It was hard to register the sound of the office door opening while I lived in the surety of my own doom. It wasn't until a young man's voice said, "Ruth," that I gasped a breath before darkness could close in, the big, white sneaker and nasty purple ropes of vein turning away from me, the corner of her lab coat brushing the desk.

"Pitch. Twice now you show your face when you know not to come here." She sounded grim and a little anxious. Also hard to discern from my own sheer terror, but I managed.

"We didn't get to talk the other day," he said. "We need to discuss the evolution of our arrangement." He came across so slick while I shivered and hugged my knees and wished I'd never come here.

"Idiot boy," she snarled, heading away from me, toward him, out the door, closing it behind her before she spoke again. I heard only muffled talking from there, a second door opening and closing and the sound of their voices traveling. Away from me until silence reined.

I was either the luckiest girl in the world or—

My phone made a few final, quick snaps of the piles of paperwork, then of the bag of drugs before I scrambled out of there, sweating and clearly looking guilty of something. But no one shouted after me as I pushed out the doors and ran for my car. No one pursued me when I peeled out of there or followed me in another car while I raced for home.

Five minutes later, panting, hands trembling, I examined the images I took and breathed in relief. Clear. Thank heavens for autofocus and the latest smart phone's incredible camera. If I'd risked that for blurry images, I would have kicked myself all the way back to New York.

Someone knocked on the passenger glass of my car and I screamed for real this time. Pitch peeked in, grinning, helping himself to the handle and scooting inside, closing it behind him. My car instantly reeked of weed but I didn't argue, turning toward him with the distinct need to hug him in his future.

"Alicia called me," he shrugged. "Big sis figured you'd run into trouble and could use some backup." He looked suddenly sad. "She's a good kid and I owe her. So."

"Thanks for the rescue," I said. "I was under the desk."

He laughed, a barking sound of derision. "I know," he said. "I was watching you." He winked. "Idiot."

Well, he was right so I wasn't about to argue. "You're going to get in a lot of trouble for this." I showed him my phone, then thought better of it, but he shrugged like it didn't matter.

"Figured a relocation was imminent," he said. "That new sheriff don't have the kind of look the other way, turn his cheek kind of attitude your dad had." Pitch met my eyes with his, that young gaze old beyond measure. "Not that the old POPO let me get away with anything. But he trusted me when no one else did."

Fair enough.

"I never meant to get Alicia into trouble," Pitch said, sounding his age at last. He fiddled with the zipper on his jacket, lean hands scarred and lined and dirty. "She took care of me when Mom and Dad died, did her best. But I didn't want to be handled, you read me?" I nodded, understanding completely. I'd run away from being handled myself. "Not her fault I'm a jackass, got into trouble. But it is my fault she got dragged in with me." Maturity from a young drug dealer? Family could make you stronger or drive you nuts. Guess he decided on the former. "I'm going to take all the heat so she's okay. Sheriff'll back me. Sissy deserves a better life than I've let her have."

I nodded, not sure what else to say. Pitch drew a deep breath then grinned as if this had all been a grand joke and he was just delivering the punchline.

"Guess I'm out," he said. "See you. Or not."

Pitch climbed out of my car, slammed the door. Waved through the glass. Vanished into the darkness. And I let him go. Because what else was I going to do for a brother that loved his sister and saved a stranger's behind when I needed it?

Daisy wrinkled her nose at the scent of me but didn't comment, hugging me anyway. Before I could explain I hadn't been smoking anything illegal, she grabbed her purse and blew me a kiss.

"Thanks, Daisy," I said, unable to find the words to tell anyone what just happened anyway.

She grinned. "Any time." And was gone. Leaving me alone with a house full of guests and a very unhappy pug who pretended she wasn't delighted to see me for about three whole seconds. Then, Petunia bounded to me and bounced about like a puppy for a moment before promptly sitting on my feet.

Pugs.

The B&B printer did a great job of reproducing the images I'd taken. I was surprised how many I'd managed to nab. I recalled having seconds, flying through the sheets, but in the end I had a good thirty solid shots of repeated paperwork that even I as a layperson could tell were not on the up and up. Worst, the fact of the matter, from what I could tell in my Google research of some of the drugs listed, Ruth had been sending the real ones out into the street and giving the nursing home residents the equivalent of placebos.

I'd take these to Crew in the morning and he could handle the rest. That was, just after he put me in a jail cell and threw away the key. Sigh. I could always just mail them to him anonymously? Right, like he wouldn't know who'd sent them.

My dark kitchen wasn't helping my mood any. I stood there in the quiet for a long moment, furious with Ryan for playing me, with Pete for playing the people of Reading, at Ruth for causing real harm to the patients she was meant to care for. Fury made me shake all over, until I hurried into my room and collapsed on my bed before I fell down.

Curling on my side felt like the right thing to do, fetal position comforting. The soft grunt of the unhappy pug pushed me up off the comforter and to the closet. I fetched the special stairs my grandmother had made for her, tucked them against the side of the bed and lay down again. A moment later, creaking and groaning her way toward me, Petunia launched herself into my arms and threw herself down with her head in the crook of my shoulder, wet nose against my cheek.

She sighed happily and promptly fell asleep while I lay awake for a long time, listening to her snore and snort, feeling her run in her dreams with high pitched yips of delight, farting her carefree canine way through the night.

And actually felt better for the pug snuggle.

CHAPTER THIRTY-FIVE

I FELT LIKE A bit of a stalker hanging out by a big tree and trying not to be noticed while the black clothed family of Pete Wilkins put his remains in the ground. Now that I knew how much his son and wife hated him though the lack of tears didn't seem so out of place.

Nor did the idea Aundrea might have murdered her husband.

I had no idea how much time I had left. The state troopers could be here any second now, though they hadn't, obviously, protested the funeral. It was already Wednesday and Crew said midweek, didn't he? I'd put off delivering the file with the photos to him in favor of lurking at the cemetery, because procrastination and I were besties.

And now I was beginning to think Crew was full of crap, had been trying to intimidate me into telling him what I knew because why would the state troopers wait this long to come if they intended to investigate at all? Which I'd been trying to do from the start, so he could go take a flying leap if he thought I would confess to a crime I didn't commit just because the big boys were getting involved. Which, apparently, they weren't.

Lying ass. Just like most men I knew. At least now it was clear where I stood. Vivian could have him.

While Jared and I had bonded over his father's crimes, I wasn't about to join the mourners or anything, making sure I kept my distance out of respect if nothing else. Though I had to come because I really needed to talk to Aundrea and, as horrible as that made me, I knew today of all days she'd be the most likely to let things slip.

Yeah, I sucked.

I wasn't the only lurker apparently, Pamela Shard hovering past a large tombstone with a towering angel on it in her dark suit and her frown, though despite her job as a reporter she didn't have a camera with her or a notebook out. I watched her watching Aundrea and had a thought even as the funeral service wrapped up—the handful of mourners drifting away quickly as if they'd only come because they had to—leaving Jared and Aundrea to make their way to their car alone.

Even the minister hurried off. I wondered if Pete had something on her, too. Probably. What secrets lay beneath the bubbling adorableness of Reading? I guess if my life was going to continue in this vein I'd likely find out.

I probably shouldn't have felt a thrill of excitement at that prospect and shrugged it off. Jared spoke to his mother a moment who waved him away. I held my place, watching him drive past, staying out of sight while Aundrea then turned and headed for the tombstone where Pamela had been waiting but had disappeared from the shadow of.

I followed, head down, trying to be discreet, circling to follow Aundrea's retreating back. She continued down the row of headstones to the far end of the cemetery, where the large marble tombs stood, only a few and obviously old, the mausoleums long left unused. She disappeared behind the first one and

I eased around the corner for a peek, not surprised to find her in Pamela's arms.

Confirming then my guess as to what Pete had to hold over his wife. Especially when the two then exchanged a passionate kiss that made me blush with the intimacy of it. I almost retreated, wanting to leave the women to their private moment, but Pamela pulled away and spotted me, grimacing to Aundrea who tensed, face tight with anxiety.

I held up both hands, approached as if they were deer in headlights terrified and ready to run. Except only Aundrea seemed afraid. Pamela looked irritated.

"How dare you." Gone was the helpful newswoman who'd come to Petunia's. She trembled a little, taking Aundrea's hand while the widow of Peter Wilkins looked down as if she were about to jerk herself free. "This has nothing to do with you."

"I know," I said, keeping my voice soothing and soft. "I'm sorry to intrude. But you have to admit, this doesn't look good for either one of you." I really was an asshole, Aundrea's face falling while Pamela gazed at her like she'd been kicked to the curb one too many times. "I'm aware of the fact Pete was blackmailing you, Mrs. Wilkins," I said, opting for the respectful address instead of going for familiarity.

"And now I know just what he was holding over your head."

Aundrea nodded, free hand swiping at tears trickling down her cheeks. Now she cried. "He knew I was gay when we were teenagers," she said. Choked a moment. "Made me marry him or he'd tell everyone. I've lived a life of hell for thirty years thanks to that man." She looked up then, defiant and furious. "I'm not sorry he's dead. But I didn't kill him if that's what you're thinking."

"I'm her alibi," Pamela said, tugging Aundrea closer. The widow didn't fight her, tucking into her welcoming embrace. "We were together that night. All night."

"Aundrea." My heart ached for her, throat tight with unshed tears. "Why did you stay?"

She shook her head. "You don't understand. My family and their position in this town." She tossed a used tissue at the marble tomb we stood next to. Right, she was a Patterson, one of the founding families and the bankroll behind a lot of the developments in Reading, equestrian center and ski lodge among them. "If they found out I'd be ostracized, I'd lose everything." She shook then, weeping openly. "My father," she could barely speak but kept going with Pamela's support, "conspired with Peter. As long as I stayed married to him I kept my trust fund. But if I ever left him—even to be alone—I'd be bereft and cut off."

All the more reason to truly hate Pete and her family, too. How charming.

"As for me," Pamela said, "Pete found out about us when we were teenagers." She winced. "I was the reason Aundrea is in this situation in the first place."

"It wasn't your fault, darling," the widow said, touching her lover's face gently, smiling a little. "You and my dear Jared have been the only lights in my life all this time."

Pamela glared at me. "Pete controlled what I published, threatening Aundrea." She shrugged angrily. "The exposé I was writing, I've been planning it a long time. But I've never been able to tell anyone what I learned, not even your father. Not until I knew Aundrea was safe." She lowered her voice, her entire body shifting from powerful anger to despair. "I couldn't care less about me, but I wouldn't let him hurt the woman I love."

Rocks and hard places came to mind. "I'm so sorry," I said. "Now that he's dead, what happens to your fortune, Aundrea?"

She snuffled, shrugged. "Some of it goes back to the family. But the bulk is still under control of his estate," she said. "Which means Jared." She smiled then, a real smile, making her look beautiful again and far younger than the years she carried. "So I suppose I'm free at last. Which makes you suspect me all the more."

"I already told her I'm your alibi," Pamela said.

"But a smart girl like the daughter of our old sheriff surely knows the two of us could have done it together." Aundrea kissed Pamela softly before smiling at me again. "Right?"

Maybe I was a sucker for a happy couple who could finally be together, but I knew she didn't do it.

"You were fighting with Ruth last night," I said. Hesitated as I realized blurting that out meant she now knew I'd been snooping. But Aundrea just sighed.

"I want out," she said. "Of all of it. I never knew the details, not really, though I was aware Peter was into some horrible things. I always hoped your father would be successful in his case but with Judge Anderson being blackmailed… well, it was clear to me from the beginning Peter wouldn't be held accountable."

A judge, huh? No wonder Dad's case fell apart if he was being undermined by the court meant to bring Pete to justice. I'd have to tell Dad.

"And what about Ruth?" Maybe this was bad timing but Aundrea was talking and seemed willing to go on. "Won't she try to blackmail you now?"

Pamela hugged Aundrea protectively. "Let her try."

"No, Fiona is right." Aundrea snuffled, pulled herself upright. "I'll just have to face my family's judgment and the public outrage."

"And that's so important, isn't it?" Pamela sounded suddenly sad, devastated really.

Aundrea flinched, sagged. "My darling—"

And the reality struck me then, just how tragic this really was. Aundrea could have walked away. Yes, it would have meant leaving all that money behind, but she could have figured something out. Been happy with Pamela. Trusted their love. Instead, she'd chosen to suffer, for them both to suffer, all these years because of money and public perception.

Not my problem and I hoped it wouldn't drive an ultimate spike between these two. They had earned happiness as far as I could tell.

"Aundrea," I said. "Did Ruth kill Pete?"

She hesitated, shrugged. "I don't know for sure," she said. "He had enough enemies out there it could be anyone. But if I had to choose…" She met Pamela's sad eyes. "Yes, if anyone could kill him, it was his hideous sister."

CHAPTER THIRTY-SIX

THE PHONE WAS RINGING when I walked into the foyer, Daisy handing it off to me almost instantly. She made a funny face, a little worried, so I knew instantly who it was when I sighed into the receiver.

"What do you want, Crew?"

Silence a moment and I wondered if I pegged it wrong before he spoke, enough anger in his voice I knew I hadn't gotten away with my little investigation.

"I just had two people walk into my office," he said. "Pamela Shard and Aundrea Wilkins. They alibied each other. Told me lots of things." He huffed softly on the other end of the line and I could see in my mind's eye his forehead vein popping out, cheeks darkening. "Mainly, that you're responsible for their appearance. Because you didn't listen, you never listen, apparently, when a police officer tells you to stay the hell away from the crimes he's investigating."

"Again," I said, so over his attitude, "you're welcome. Because you really think they would have come to you otherwise?"

Enough silence followed he knew I was right and oh boy did he hate it.

"I have more to tell you if you're willing to listen," I said.

"Just spill it," he snarled, the sound of his chair squeaking a clear indication he was paying attention.

I told him about the key, about Dad and Alicia, knowing I was betraying my father all over again but unable to stop myself. And rushed on to fill him in on the files, the photos I took. He hummed and tsked and grunted often enough I knew he was still there, and was likely writing down all the charges he was going to lay against me so he could lock me away forever.

By the time I was done, whispering now while Daisy smilingly helped some guests with questions about Reading, Crew actually sounded rather calm.

"Ruth is the best fit," he said. "I've already come to that conclusion. And I'm well aware your father's been continuing his own investigation. I've been in touch with the people he met the night Pete Wilkins died."

"And you no longer think I killed him?" That was a relief.

"I'd be so lucky," he grumbled. "No, Fee. I told you before, I don't. But the evidence you found is illegal, you must know that."

"But you can use it as leverage against her, can't you?" Damn it, I really messed up, didn't I?

"Listen." He sounded tired again, worn out. "I do appreciate your help." Sure he did. "And you've broken a few things open for me with your stumbling around that I wouldn't have managed on my own thanks to the people of this ridiculous town." So he was frustrated with his new job, was he? Dad grew up here, so I guess it was easier for him. But I knew very well an outsider would be handled rather than welcomed, so he had to be struggling. And that meant I should be showing a little compassion instead of being a pain in his butt. "Ruth and Pete were having business troubles from what I've uncovered." Wow, he was sharing? "Ruth registered three shell companies linked back to her and the nursing home in the last four weeks. She's been siphoning funds into those accounts. While I can't use your evidence, it's clear from what you found she had the means and the motive. But she has an alibi for the night of Pete's murder."

Well, crappy. "What alibi?"

"Footage taken from the nursing home of her in her office." He was still talking, amazing.

"The time code could be altered. She has access to all her own security footage, I assume." Did that mean there was video of me breaking in? Whoops.

Crew sighed. "That's exactly what I was thinking. So she's also smack dab in opportunity." Finally, we were getting somewhere. "But Fee, I really need you to step back, okay? I'm looking at Ruth right now. And if you alert her to the fact I'm doing so, she could destroy evidence or bolt and we'll lose her."

Honestly, I didn't care if she was ever persecuted for the murder of her brother. They were both vile creatures who deserved what they got and karma had a way of sneaking up on you and smacking you down. So I felt a great sense of relief as I smiled into the phone, hoping he could hear the expression in my voice.

"I'm done," I said. "Go get her, tiger."

Crew laughed, shaky and weary. "I'm not going to survive this job," he said. "Or you Flemings. But I'm going to try." And he hung up.

I turned, a huge weight lifting from my shoulders as Daisy waved goodbye to the departing guests before spinning to ward me with her eyes huge and full lips parted in anticipation.

I hugged her, bouncing a little, so happy to have everything wrapped up. Daisy giggled and let me go while I bent to pat Petunia on the head and she panted at me in obvious happiness.

"Good news?" Daisy's smile was infectious.

"The best," I said.

She handed me a long, white envelope. A quick glance at the label said Wilkins Construction, Inc. A faint frown pulled at the line between my eyes, but when I ripped it open, heart beating a little too fast, I found a beaming smile replaced it while I skimmed the contents.

"Jared," I said, moisture rimming my eyes, making it hard to read his signature. And the details.

But I caught enough to look up at Daisy and hug the letter to my chest. "He signed Petunia's back to me," I whispered. "With his thanks." And tracked the funds Ryan placed in the account under my name, all the way back to him and his firm.

Daisy squealed so loud I flinched and then hugged me until my ribs creaked while my pug—as much as I was her human—barked and spun in happy circles as if she understood completely just how awesome this moment turned out to be.

CHAPTER THIRTY-SEVEN

DAD'S SMILE TOLD ME everything I needed to know, Mom hugging me around the shoulders before offering Petunia another slice of banana. It disappeared down the pug's throat while I continued to beam as I had since the moment I opened Jared's letter.

"He said if I ever decide to sell, let him know," I told them. "But fake signature or not, he's not contesting anything and just wants to clean up his father's mess."

"Jared's always been a good kid," Dad said.

"And poor Aundrea and Pamela." Mom tsked as she wiped her fingers from the last of the banana while Petunia managed to look starving despite her portly figure. "How horrible for both of them." She patted my hand. "I went to school with the girls and it was honestly no secret."

"Well, Aundrea clearly thought it was a big deal," I said.

Dad sat back, arms crossing over his chest. "You say Crew already knew I'd been out of town?"

I winked at him. "Guess he's okay at doing his job after all, Dad."

My father grunted. "We'll see."

After a slice of celebratory apple pie Mom insisted on baking, I wandered home again with Petunia huffing beside me, her round belly full of scraps I wished my parents hadn't fed her. They wouldn't have to deal with her flatulence later.

"Okay, here's the new rules," I told her. "You can sleep on the bed, but no more stuff that's bad for you. Or my nose." She waddled and panted and didn't argue. "And I promise I'll take you on more walks and try not to leave you home so much."

That seemed to suit her just fine.

My only job remaining? Call a lawyer. Because thanks to Jared's information, it was time to kick Ryan's ass all the way to prison. That would make this entire mess wrap up in the very best way possible.

The B&B was quiet when I got back, Mary and Betty in the kitchen as I poked my head inside. They both looked up, flinched, glanced away again. At least there weren't any more stares or glares or accusatory looks. But I really needed to talk to them and was finally in the mood to do it.

No time like the present, right?

"Ladies." I unhooked Petunia's harness but she just sat on my feet anyway and didn't leave me while I spoke. "I think we got off to a bad start. I swept in here after Grandmother Iris died with no idea what I was doing and put all of the weight on your shoulders." I really didn't think I had, but if I'd learned anything it was sugar went down easier than vinegar. And the way they both perked seemed to confirm I was on the right track. "I appreciate so much the fact you kept this place running when she was so ill and even after her death without thanks or anyone to support you." That much was true and they both nodded, their sullen anger seemed gone at last. Wicked. Was I really on a roll? "I want you to know you both do an amazing job and I'm so glad you're here to help me." I surprised myself when I realized I wasn't bending the truth to make them feel better. Sure, their attitudes weren't the best, but this place ran like clockwork, to the point I really didn't have the kind of headaches I'd thought might come up. "Okay, your turn," I said. "Because I want to hear what you have to say."

Betty poked her sister and, as per their arrangement, Mary spoke. "We were afraid you were going to fire us," she said. And they both burst into tears.

Well, that wasn't what I was expecting and was so close to the truth it hit me like a ton of very heavy bricks. Petunia ambled forward while I rushed to them and hugged the pair of them, heart breaking. I guided the older ladies onto stools and squeezed their hands, while they snuffled and bobbed their gray heads.

"We adored your grandmother," Mary said, wiping at her round cheeks. "And when she fell ill, we did everything we could to make sure Petunia's stayed up to her level of excellence while she was sick."

I nodded. "You did a great job."

"Then she died." That last word came out as a wail while Betty sobbed twice before falling still.

"And you came. And we didn't know you and you were so quick and irritated and out of sorts and we didn't know what to do."

Totally a fair assessment. I'd barged in here like a house on fire, wanting to prove something to myself. And made them miserable.

"Can we agree to start again?" I looked back and forth between them. "I love it here, I never thought I would. And I'm so happy to tell you Jared Wilkins cancelled the claim on this place, so we're good to go."

They both lurched toward me and hugged me so fast I staggered back, Petunia barking her delight while they crushed me in their strong arms. Wow, they were a powerful pair for old ladies. I needed to stop underestimating them.

"That's wonderful, Fiona," Mary said, smiling through her tears. Then paused, looked down at her hands while Betty patted her back. "You're not going to fire us, then?" She peeked up at me through her wet lashes, her perfect bun falling loose in places from the enthusiasm of her hug.

"Why would I do that?" I embraced them both in turn and resigned myself to the fact I'd have them here no matter what. "I need you two. For as long as you want to stay." And paused. "But, I need to know you have my back. And that a few changes I'd like to make won't be cause for rebellion."

A short staff meeting commenced where I outlined my plans to take full advantage of how busy things were. That a lunch and early afternoon tea menu would lure our guests home again. The two were so bubbly excited I half expected Betty to talk. Yeah, no such luck. But we parted as friends, my heart lighter than it had been in years. Well, if I was going to be honest, than it had been my entire life. I ducked downstairs to my apartment for a few minutes to catch my breath and take the time I needed to absorb just how awesome my life had suddenly become.

From cheated on ex-girlfriend who fled her old existence and almost lost her future to a swindling dead guy to happy B&B owner with her whole future ahead of her.

I'd take it.

CHAPTER THIRTY-EIGHT

THE SHOE BOX PEGGY brought me caught my eye, lured me in. I sat at the island in my kitchen, looking at last through the rest of the contents, at the photos of them as girls together, more memorabilia from trips they'd taken, from their time at school. At the bottom, tucked into a corner, sat a cute little toy that squeaked endearingly when I squeezed its small ducky body.

"Cookie must have accidentally sent us a gift," I smiled at Petunia whose head cocked to the side at the sound. "I'd give it to you but you'd wreck it in about two seconds." She loved to chew anything she could get her teeth on, and I'd lost enough shoes my first few days to prove it. "Let's run this over to

Peggy and Cookie, shall we? I'm sure they'd love to have it back." And see us. It seemed like perfect timing to go have tea now that I was on the right track.

Instead of going out the front door and around the sidewalk, I exited out the back, into the garden and to the fence. It wasn't hard to find the space between the carriage house and the wooden slats of the barrier where Peggy and Cookie slipped through so the little dog could crap in my bushes. It seemed so petty now, the fact I'd ever intended to say a word about it. Let Cookie poop. She was in good Petunia company and her crap was way smaller than the pug's, after all.

Peggy's back yard was a bit overgrown, less English country garden than mine and more gone off on its own accord. I followed the path to the back door, grinning to myself as I glanced to the right and spotted the small set of steps next to the fence. And now I knew what she stood on to talk to me over the barrier. Dedicated neighbor, you betcha.

She'd be shocked to find me coming through here. This would be all I'd have to do to tip her off. She'd know I knew about Cookie's poop trips and we'd have a laugh at the joke. A whimsical sense of goodwill washed through me while Petunia paused on the porch and stared suddenly, panting halted, head tilted and a low growl escaping her.

I hesitated at her reaction and only then heard voices coming from inside. I stared through the back door into Peggy's kitchen, caught sight down the hall of two people, one tiny and slim, the other hulking over her and lurched for the handle, jerking it open.

It didn't occur to me to worry about what I was walking into, not when Peggy, Cookie nowhere to be seen, turned with her lined face pale in shock as Ruth Wilkins raised one hand to her.

Thank goodness I'd brought my cell phone, fishing it out of my back pocket and dialing 9-1-1 for the second time in less than a week. Peggy sobbed, hunching forward, arms rising to protect herself from the big woman's threatening blow.

"Don't touch her," I snarled, phone still ringing, damn it. "I'm calling the police."

Ruth laughed, booming and obscene. "You have no idea what you're doing," she growled. "Get out of here and mind your own business."

"Not so good at that," I shot back. Petunia woofed, scuttling sideways, her big body turning then to face us while she growled softly, and only then did

I spot poor shaking Cookie tucked under the kitchen table behind the pug who protected her with her bulky body. No one answered the emergency call while Ruth lumbered toward me. I hit redial but my finger slipped and instead called Crew.

Well, probably a good thing.

I heard him pick up as I shouted at Ruth. "Don't come any closer. And leave Peggy Munroe alone, Ruth Wilkins."

She grunted herself to a halt, stared down at the cell phone in my hand, scowled at me then. Surely Crew got the hint? Meanwhile, the looming woman leaned in toward me, her beady eyes the same as her brother's but a threat in her expression so powerful I was sure, now, she'd killed Pete and probably in cold blood.

"Please, Ruth, just go. I don't have anything for you, I swear." Peggy met my eyes, her hands fumbling for something by the kitchen door. "You and Peter were always my favorite grandnephew and niece, you know that." They were *what*?

Ruth boomed another laugh, spinning on her elderly great aunt. "You old bat," she snapped. "Pete might have fallen for your kindly old lady act, but I didn't." She ignored me this time, heading for Peggy whose hands had stilled, grasping something I couldn't see while I tucked my phone into my pocket and prepared to leap on her back to keep her away from my neighbor. "Now, tell me where it is. I know it's here somewhere."

Before I could react, Peggy shrieked like a banshee and swung, her old arms shaking, the cane she'd grasped from its place by the door impacting the sides of Ruth's knees. The big woman shouted in shock and fell sideways, hitting her head on the counter before collapsing to the floor, her eyes rolling back into her head.

For a brief instant Peggy looked triumphant, like a hunter who'd finally downed her prey. Then, she dropped the cane and burst into tears, her hands over her face. I hurried to her, circling Ruth's unconscious body, hugging the dear old lady to me while she clung to me and trembled.

"They were threatening me," she whispered. "Wanted my house, to put me in the nursing home." She met my eyes, hers bloodshot and her face drawn and ashen from her ordeal. "I was so afraid. You saved me, Fee."

I laughed shakily as a siren wailed closer, the cavalry on the way. "I think you saved yourself, Peggy. Thinking about taking up baseball?"

We giggled together in near hysteria as the front door at the end of the hall burst open and Crew and Robert rushed in. Too late to help, but still welcome. The wide eyed stare he gave me could have been respect or accusation, but I couldn't care less which.

"Book her, Crew," I said, nodding at the fallen Wilkins. "Attempted assault of her own great auntie."

CHAPTER THIRTY-NINE

I SAT WITH PEGGY who rocked Cookie in her lap, the little bow on the top of her head gone missing in the fracas. Petunia perched on Peggy's other side, nudging the nervous little dog every once in a while with her wet nose. Crew and Robert talked at the entry to the sitting room while a stretcher wheeled past, Ruth's silent form laid out on it as the paramedics took her away.

"Still out cold," Crew said, nodding to Peggy. "You're okay, Mrs. Munroe?"

"I will be, dear," she said, patting my hand that rested on her arm, "with help and time. Horrible woman. She and Peter, too." She shuddered. "I don't know what happened to those two to make them so hateful. They were my Daniel's family, you know. There was a time I would have loved to call them my own. We weren't blessed with children, you see." She wept then, leaning on my shoulder. "I've been so afraid of them for so long, it's lovely to know they're gone."

"You said they were looking for something?" Crew hesitated, waited.

Peggy looked up, snuffling, nodded. "They were searching for the deed to my house," she said. "Going on about power of attorney and how I can't take care of myself anymore." Sounded familiar enough, though their own blood didn't warrant a fake signature, just a snatch and grab. I guess she showed them. Or Ruth, anyway. I know I wouldn't want to mess with her. "I can show you." She made as if to move but fell back into the cushions, weak and shaking.

"That's all right," Crew said. "You can share details with me later. Why did they want the deed?"

Like he didn't know. Still, I suppose he had to ask. Peggy shrugged, sagging into me. "To steal my property from me and put me in the home for good. Peter was at least kind about it even though he was a terrible fraud. But Ruth, she is a bully." The old lady's jaw set. "They tried to steal Petunia's from Iris, did you know that?"

I loved her outrage. "All taken care of."

She exhaled her relief. "I know, that young Jared. Nothing like his father." She nodded abruptly. "I'm pressing charges, blood or no blood."

"Of course." Crew met my eyes, his widening slightly as if trying to deliver a message. "Maybe after you get checked out at the hospital Fee can bring you to the station to file a report."

"I'm fine, dear, really," she said. "I don't need a doctor. She didn't get to touch me. Not with Fee barging in like my hero." She smiled at me, tremulous and sad. "Thank you, dear."

"Any time," I said, "but hopefully never again."

"Amen to that."

Crew left, Robert with him, the paramedics gone with Ruth in the back of the ambulance. I hugged Peggy around the shoulders, feeling the quiet of her house settle around us, the faint ticking of the big clock in her foyer counting the seconds that stretched into the afternoon.

"Can I make you some tea, Peggy?" I needed to do something, the tension of the last little while making me antsy to release the adrenaline buildup.

"Thank you, dear." Peggy leaned back, eyes closing, Cookie tucking her nose under her tail as she curled up. "I really am very tired. That would be lovely."

I stood, headed for the door and the hall. Noticed a bowl had been knocked over by the front door and went to fetch it. Ribbons, tiny colored slips of velvet, all for Cookie's topknot. Pink and orange and green and…

Red.

I froze, heart pounding. Then shrugged it off. The red scrap of fabric in Fat Benny's mouth. That's where it had come from. Probably fell off when Cookie was using my garden as a bathroom. So not evidence of the murder at all. Right?

But the little dog only ever pooped by the fence and that was on the other side of the yard. I fingered the strips of velvet, mind beginning to spin. Well, the wind could have carried it into the water, and the koi were such idiots, they'd eat anything.

Silly. I obviously needed time away from mysteries because I was making them up in my head, now. Like the cane Peggy carried and how much the rubber bottom was about the size of an old fashioned ketchup bottle, ridges matching the ones in the hole near the pond…

"Put it together then, have you?"

I spun around, the bowl still in my hands, crouching over the fallen bits of fabric, staring down the hall at the silhouette of Peggy watching me. She didn't seem so vulnerable anymore. If anything, the old lady loomed as much as Ruth had, threatening despite her small size. Holding her cane against her. My eyes traveled down to the base, to the perfect round tip. I was right. Just like the impression in the dirt beside the scuff mark where Pete slipped.

"You hit him with your cane." The bruise Crew mentioned. On Pete's leg. Perimortem but fresh, as if it hadn't had time to develop before he died, evolved after he'd drowned. "He fell and hit his head."

"But he didn't die, the big idiot." Not a trace of weariness or any sort of kindness in those words. I heard a click, looked up again, found the barrel of a gun in my face. And knew I'd been off track from minute one. "He was supposed to *die*."

"So you used your cane to roll him into the water." Where he drowned.

She shrugged her narrow shoulders, Cookie trotting out of the room behind her to sit shaking at

Peggy's feet. No sign of Petunia. My heart clenched, worry hitting me hard between the shoulders. What had she done to my pug? Sure, here I was with a gun pointed at me and I was worried about Petunia.

"Worked on Peter," she said. "Figured it would work on that hideous cow, Ruth, too." She leveled the barrel at me, obviously practiced with a gun.

"Why? Why kill him?" Not that it mattered, I guess. While I looked my death in the face and realized I was a terrible detective no matter what I thought otherwise.

She laughed. "You think either of those two morons had the mental capacity to run an operation as complex as this one?" Peggy's disdain felt surreal, like I'd fallen into a film noir and stood on a cliff's edge with my doom pending. "Please. The entire operation was mine. Has been for years. And those ungrateful brats," she thudded the hardwood floor with the rubber end of her cane for emphasis, "thought they could muscle in on my carefully constructed process."

Wow. Just, wow.

The photo on the top of the pile, from the shoe box she'd given me. The image of her with Grandmother Iris was of the sofa in the foyer of the nursing home. And the old man I'd seen her with, he was another victim, wasn't he? "You were getting the signatures from the dying." How sick.

"The latest of my schemes," she shrugged. "Was lucrative until Pete got greedy and started mining still in towners. People with loved ones hanging around. Fake signatures, the fool. I only ever accepted the real thing."

"And Ruth's drug thefts? You had nothing to do with that?"

"I wouldn't say that." Peggy took a step forward, Cookie hovering at her feet. Still no Petunia. My heart broke, mind imagining her lying in the sitting room, dead or injured, unable to come to me. And anger shattered any remaining fear. I stood up while Peggy's aim didn't waver. "I took advantage of the situation once my stupid grandniece admitted what she was up to. But that had to end. Too risky." She wrinkled her nose, looking ridiculous suddenly, an old woman, tiny and frail in a faded dress holding a gun like she knew how to use it. "Too messy." She stopped, stared at me with the most calculating expression. "Peter didn't want to set up his son, but it was the only way. Your darling ex-boyfriend, Ryan is it? Gave me the idea. When we found out he was embezzling and set you up for the blame." She laughed again, a solid cackle. "He's a deplorable boy, dear. You really can do better."

"You wanted the B&B, didn't you?" The gleam in her eyes told me as much, the way her thin mouth tightened.

"Damn that old witch, she wouldn't sign." Peggy thudded her cane again, hand with the gun twitching enough I felt anxiety return. "Pete chose the fake signature, though I told him not to. But I owed your grandmother a thing or two, dear Fiona. So I let him do it."

The box. "Why give me that box of photos, of her things?" How did that make sense?

"I had to know what you knew, of course," she said. "And Iris, well, she never suspected we weren't the best of friends, did she?" Her snort carried disdain. "She really was a fool. Like your father who never suspected me, not for a moment." She obviously thought that a great joke.

"But, why was Pete in my yard that night?" The last piece of this insane puzzle.

"Some foolishness Iris told him on her deathbed," Peggy snorted. "About a treasure she buried. He just couldn't wait. The moron." She snarled at the floor a moment as if remembering. “He came here first, looking for—”

I waited as she grunted. “The same thing Ruth was looking for today?”

The prompting worked, the old woman exhaling in frustrated impatience. “Not like it matters now,” she said. “You’re dead anyway. Yes, he came for my ledger. The one I keep with evidence of all my business dealings.” Peggy’s hand wavered slightly. Was she getting tired? “Ruth thought she could bully me if she got her hands on it, just like Pete did. But he was far easier to manipulate than she ever was.” She waved the gun at me. “That night, when I told him where he could go, he grumbled about not needing me anymore, some foolish hidden treasure and slipped through the fence. I went after him to chase him off. The last thing we needed was any kind of attention at that point.” I could only imagine. He took a risk wandering around like that. One guest up at the wrong time and he’d be under scrutiny. “He was going to drop the bank account blackmail information on you when you came to protest the signature.” Peggy did smile then, a horrible expression devoid of humanity. “I wished I could have been there!” She licked her lips, grin tightening before it fell. "He had to make trouble, didn't he? Argue with me over who was running the show. Threaten to cut me out." A little shrug, a bit of a brush off. "Doesn't matter. I took care of him and I'll have Petunia's now anyway. Once you're dead, that is."

"How you figure?" I couldn't move, couldn't think, stuck with a gun in my face and no alternatives. I couldn't even reach my phone in my back pocket without her seeing. Stupid, stupid. How could I have missed this?

"Ruth knows to keep her mouth shut and take the fall or I'll make her life even more miserable than it's already set up to be." Peggy's grin tightened. "And your parents will happily sell with you gone, I'm sure of it. I can convince that weakling boy, Jared, to buy the property for me. And then everything will be done." Another cackle. "Round about, but perfect all the same."

"What did Grandmother Iris do to you?" They'd looked like such friends in the photos.

"It doesn't matter," Peggy snapped. "Now, I'm done talking and you're still alive. Something I need to rectify."

"You can't just shoot me," I said, holding up both hands. "They'll arrest you for murder."

"Who, me?" Peggy's voice dropped to a trembling whisper, her face morphing to weakness and despair. "But, I was so afraid after my horrible grandniece was here and my husband's old gun, well. I keep it for protection. Fee left, went home. I had no idea she'd come back. I thought she was an intruder and I… I…" She sobbed twice before stilling completely, voice cold. "I shot her thinking she was a burglar. Who could blame me after everything I've been through?"

In that moment I knew she'd get away with it. And that I was toast.

A fawn bundle of fur with black ears and a growl like a demon lurched from the sitting room, hitting Peggy in the back of the knees and driving her to the floor. She cried out, Cookie darting out of the way and I lunged, disarming the old woman with a quick twist of my wrist, hand grasping the barrel and jerking it loose from her grasp.

I might not have been in law enforcement, but Dad taught me to handle a gun.

Peggy snarled at me, swiped with her cane, but I was already dialing, weapon trained on her while

Petunia limped to my side, sinking to sit on my feet, a cut over her right eye seeping blood.

"You're going down, Peggy," I said. "For all of it."

She tried, I'll give her that, face settling into her fragile old lady act. But I wasn't having any, Crew answering as I spoke.

"Point a gun at me, fine," I said. "But you tried to kill my dog, you bitch. You're done."

CHAPTER FORTY

IT WAS EASY TO smile at the adorably New England chic Mr. and Mrs. Thurston as I handed them their room keys, sunlight beaming into the foyer through the open door. I watched the happy young couple while they climbed the stairs to their room, ooh and ahhing over my place in their excitement to be here. Chatter from the dining room drifted toward me, the soft sounds of pots and pans in the kitchen while Betty whipped up fresh biscuits for afternoon tea, our second so far this week and met with great excitement by locals and tourists alike. The murder had added to our reach and notoriety and thanks to Daisy updating our social media with the successful resolution of Pete Wilkins's death we'd seen a huge surge in followers and calls for new bookings.

Who knew murder was big business?

My plan to start offering little extras in the last week since Peggy's arrest and my staff's new leaf turn had made things busier around here, but I wasn't complaining. Daisy seemed to adore it, sweeping elegantly from table to table with all her charm beaming from her. Though, I wondered how long I'd get to keep her. She'd started dating someone new and was asking for more and more time off. Well, fair enough, except if I had to hire someone I really needed to look into it. August was just a week away and with no sign of things slowing down.

"Fee!" Speak of the devil, Daisy hurried from the dining room with a paper in her hands, shoving it at me with a beaming smile. "Look!"

I did, the front page exposé about Ruth, Pete and Peggy all the news in town the last few days. The state troopers had, in fact, shown up as Crew said they would—so not a liar, then—but by then he had Peggy in custody, thanks to me, and Ruth squealing on everyone involved for a deal. Not that I was a fan of deals, but if it meant taking Peggy down, I was all for it.

Petunia looked up at me from her usual place sitting on my feet. A cute little cartoon pug band aid covered the stitches over her eye, placed there—and replaced often—with loving adoration by Daisy when I brought the pug home from her vet visit shortly after Peggy's attack. No worse for wear but milking her injury for everything it was worth, Petunia happily accepted all the snacks and love and attention everyone heaped on her.

"There's my little hero," Daisy said, rubbing the pug's cheek. Petunia groaned her appreciation and I didn't argue. She'd saved my butt, so she was owed a bit of latitude.

The byline on the piece was Pamela Shard, of course, but there was a rather smug triumphant feeling to the exposé. Not that I blamed her. She and Aundrea had been getting out and about together and from what I'd heard from the ever keen Daisy, the fact no one seemed to care—or find it a surprise—they were gay was a bit of a letdown for Aundrea and a huge relief for Pamela. After years of suffering, I guess the former Mrs. Wilkins was expecting a giant disaster and got crickets. Had to rankle.

Nice they had adopted Cookie, the little dog seemingly happier than she'd ever been.

"Look, Jared, how sweet is he?" Daisy pointed to the paragraph quoting the young Wilkins heir. "*I'm already planning to return the bulk of the stolen properties to the rightful owners while offering partnerships where return isn't possible.*"

Good kid, Jared.

Alicia, from the next paragraph's information, was being credited with helping the police, but her brother, Pitch, was on the run and being sought for questioning. Any information would be kept strictly confidential and a reward was offered. Poor Pitch. He got the short end of the stick. But that's the way he played it, so I wished him well despite his criminal activities. He did right by his sister, after all.

Dad was mentioned too, to my surprise, praised for refusing to give up on the investigation after Judge Anderson was identified as colluding with Pete, being blackmailed for having a prisoner turnover arrangement with the local prison. That was another big ball of wax and from what I heard the state troopers dropped Crew's case like a rock and ran after that one before the FBI could snatch it up. And left our little town in its nice, quiet solitude—

except for the multitude of tourists, that was—once more.

The nursing home was under new management, surprise, surprise. And, the small piece under the main article announcing the sale of Jacob's Flowers caught my attention.

"Simon and Terri are splitting," Daisy said, nose wrinkling in sympathy.

Terri I could muster empathy for.

My phone rang, the cell vibrating on the side board but one glance at the number and I ignored it.

"He's still trying to talk to you?" Daisy covered her grin with one hand.

"Ryan's in a heap of trouble," I said, rather satisfied with that turn of events. The state troopers did one thing right, contacting his firm in New York before scrambling off to take down the judge. He'd been calling me in a panic ever since, but I wasn't about to let the snake have the satisfaction of trying to wheedle his way out of this. If the long, rambling apologies and fake tears he sobbed into his messages were any indication, Ryan had completely underestimated me. Sucker.

The front door opened, Vivian entering with—of all people—Crew on her arm. Well, she was on his arm, but same thing. He grimaced at me, an apology? All while the Queen of the Small Town Bakery swept past us and into my dining room. For tea. In my B&B.

On purpose, naturally. To show off the claws she had hooked firmly in our handsome sheriff. She was wasting her time. I had no interest in men right now. If ever. Still, he really did know how to work that butt.

"I'll tell her to get her ass out." Daisy fumed next to me, but I shrugged and grinned.

"It's fine," I said.

"If you say so," she grumbled. Then brightened. "I'll tell Mary to spit in her tea." She spun, full skirt swirling around her and hurried off to the kitchen before I could stop her.

The door opened again and I turned back, shocked by my next guest. Malcolm Murray entered alone, the slim, spare old Irishman looking around with a happy expression, nodding to me.

"You kept the place the same as Iris," he said, bending to pat Petunia who accepted his affection with her typical good grace. "Well done, Fiona."

I gaped at him a moment before gesturing toward the dining room. "Tea?"

He winked. "Best in town," he said. And drifted past me, pausing at the door. "You say hullo to your da for me?"

I nodded, swallowed. What was he after?

Malcolm laughed. "Excellent. Maybe I'll pop round again sometime."

And then he was gone inside and I was left panting my anxiety over whatever that was into the quiet air of the foyer.

Petunia followed me down to my apartment when Daisy returned with a smug grin. I didn't ask, just escaped for a few minutes, the same sunlight beaming into my kitchen and warming my face. I turned to pour myself some coffee and spotted the metal box, padlock hanging at a jaunty angle. And looked down at the farting pug on my feet. Of course.

It took a bit of hunting through Grandmother Iris's things, but I finally located the papers I was looking for. Petunia's birthday worked as the combination, naturally. Fingers trembling, I popped open the protesting lid, the metal grinding a bit. But the hinges worked fine once I'd wiggled the top free and the lid fell to the counter, hanging there, contents exposed.

Not treasure or money or jewels. Letters. Dozens of them. Addressed to Grandmother Iris from the most unlikely source. Daniel Munroe. Adoring husband, I could only imagine, of one Peggy next door. No wonder she hated my grandmother. Love letters hot enough to make me blush and put them aside. Did Grandmother Iris know Peggy was on to her about the affair with her husband? Questions I'd have to ask someday. For now, it didn't matter.

Because at the bottom of the box lay a key with a black plastic tag. B-562. A safety deposit box key. And another mystery to keep me going.

Daisy's call for me from upstairs broke my excited reverie. "Coming!" I closed the box, pocketing the key. Looked down at Petunia and grinned at her sweet face, the adorable band aid. And went upstairs to see to my guests.

The Reading Reader Gazette

VOLUME 1 ISSUE 1 JULY 29TH, 2017 WWW.RRGAZETTE.COM

News Briefs

1. **Parking on Main Street**: town council, led by Mayor Olivia Walker, announced yesterday that parking meters will not be installed as had been previously suggested. A vote of 9-1 against in favor of continuing free parking in al of Reading was passed to much celebration in the gallery. Mayor Walker said this victory is another win for local tourism efforts.

2. **White Valley Golf Club**: Construction quality has come under question with the allegations of building code violations by recently deceased contractor Pete Wilkins of Wilkins's Construction, Inc. Owner Jared Wilkins has assured Mayor Olivia Walker and town council he is personally investigating all matters pertaining to his father's business.

3. **Yacht Club Fundraiser**: The Reading Yacht Club will host a Pirate Night as part of an effort to revitalize the club. Guests will board a real pirate ship and sail Reading Lake in search of the fabled treasure legends claim is lost in the depths. Club President Gerald Mortimer is optimistic about the event and plans more such in the future.

4. **Reading Nursing Care**: Now under new management, Mayor Olivia Walker is delighted with the change in administration. The town council last night committed a $70,000 budget to updating the facility with promises to continue supporting residents.

Winner of this week's Fire Hall 50 50 draw: Mary Jones. Congratulations, Mary!

Please send any pending community notices to: pamela@rrgazette.com before 4PM

Murder Suspect Apprehended

Peggy Munroe of 16 Booker Street has been named in the murder of her grand-nephew, Peter Wilkins with connection to further illegal activties with her grand-niece, Ruth Wilkins

Family Ties to Criminal Activity and Murder in Reading

By Pamela Shard

The murder of Peter Wilkins has been solved with the arrest late Wednesday afternoon of local resident Peggy Jean Munroe of 16 Booker Street. Also under arrest is the deceased's sister, Ruth Anne Wilkins of 412 Primary Lane, in connection with a variety of charges relating to fraud, theft, drug misappropriation and blackmail.

Thanks to the tireless efforts of former Curtis County Sheriff John Fleming (retired) and assisted by our newly elected Sheriff Crew Turner and his deputies, a deep well of criminal activity has only begun to be plumbed. With allegations of collusion with our very own Judge Victor Anderson as well as ties to out of state suppliers to the Wilkins's Construction, Inc. company, authorities say it will take time and further careful inquiry to fully uncover the depths of the case. However, Mayor Olivia Walker and the town council are confident those responsible for wrongdoing are now in custody.

Drowned in the koi pond at Petunia's Bed and Breakfast last week, the extent of Peter Wilkins's criminal activities have only now come to light with his passing. Son and heir Jared Wilkins said, "My father's crimes will be investigated and fully uncovered while I work to make amends with victims of his illegal activities and to restore the Wilkins family name."

For the time being, the pursuit of further information remains in the hands of our own sheriff's department. It remains to be seen what, if anything further, will be discovered about the Wilkins crime ring.

Former head administrator of the Reading Nursing Care facility, Ruth Anne Wilkins, has been remanded to custody and prosecutors will request she not be allowed bail. As for murderess Peggy Jean Munroe, it has been uncovered she was, in fact, the mastermind of the illegal schemes that have plagued Reading and beyond and that the Crown prosecutor in conjunction with state police are doing everything they can to convict her.

Petunia Says:
Please review!
Thank You!

AND NOW FOR A sneak peek at Book Two of the Fiona Fleming Cozy Mystery series…

CHOCOLATE HEARTS AND MURDER

CHAPTER ONE

WHY WAS IT FANCY Valentine's Day drinks were always tinted red? Reminded me more of gore and mayhem than anything to do with romance. Which said a lot, I suppose, for my state of mind when it came to relationships and dating.

No bitterness in Fiona Fleming toward the opposite sex or anything.

I sipped carefully at the mimosa the bartender smilingly handed me and shrugged off the sweetness. It had alcohol in it, so I guess it would do. A few of these and I might even find a way to enjoy myself tonight. Yeah, right.

Don't get me wrong. It was kind of a big deal to be invited, from what I understood, to Mayor Olivia Walker's extra special, don't you dare miss it, White Valley Ski Lodge Resort Extravaganza and fashion show. Snort. I tipped my glass to a pair of young women I didn't know and perused the bar where I hoped to spend the bulk of tonight before returning to my room and hiding out there until I could go home.

My free hand tugged at the short hemline of the dress Daisy picked out for me while I did my damnedest not to show how uncomfortable I was in the shining satin sheath. No one told my best friend that redheads look terrible in crimson. Though, as it turned out, this particular dress's color actually complimented my thick, auburn hair, matched to the deep red lipstick she insisted I wear. The kind of lasts all night and won't kiss off stuff she knew was my only hope for keeping color on my lips due to my utter lack of giving a crap about makeup.

Smart girl, that Daisy.

Maybe I could carve out a little corner by the bar here, in the dim light of the long, narrow space with the lovely music piping through in tasteful strains of reworked pop songs, (sarcasm, check) while water cascaded in enthusiastic downfall over the glass feature that was the back wall. The slick marble tiles were a bit treacherous underfoot, made worse by the heels Daisy forced on my feet. Come to think of it, I'd been worried they'd be hurting by now, laughed at her when she insisted on taping my toes, only to discover she knew what she was doing and that my tender, sneaker-favoring tootsies actually felt all right.

I spotted Olivia across the room and ducked my head, the updo making it impossible to hide behind my hair like I usually did. Damn Daisy and her deft fingers, though I had to admit the final result—makeup, dress, shoes and hair—left me a little breathless. I turned toward the bar, the mirror behind it reflecting her artwork, and grinned for a second at just how hot I actually looked.

Now, if only I wasn't the only woman here under thirty who was single… not fair. I was sure it only felt that way. And nice to have an excuse to do something on Valentine's Day that had nothing to do with men or pretending they weren't all jerks. Still. I watched Olivia in her pale cream gown making her rounds, all poised politician perfection, and my grin turned to a grimace. I'd let her bully me into this, just like I'd allowed it the last eight months since I took over my Grandmother Iris's B&B, Petunia's. From the moment she intervened with the sheriff over the death of Pete Wilkins and kept my business open, murder or no murder, the woman seemed to think she owned me. And the rest of the town.

Mind you, she was doing a stellar job of putting our sleepy little Reading, Vermont on the map of must-visit places in the continental US. Savvy didn't begin to describe her ability to wrangle press and attention and everyone thrived thanks to it. But there were times it rankled.

Like three weeks ago when she showed up in the foyer of Petunia's, patted my pug of the same name on the head (a prerequisite for anyone wishing to spend even five seconds at the B&B) and then informed me in no uncertain terms I was attending tonight's little soiree.

No luck hiding from her, it turned out. With her carefully cultivated welcoming smile plastered on her olive skinned face, makeup professionally applied and hair glossy in the low light, Olivia took time out of her busy schmoozing schedule to spend a moment with me.

"A smile would be lovely," she said through her own, tone not matching her expression. "For the good of Reading." That elegant pause, weighted with guilt was by now a classic. "You *do* want our town to continue seeing success, don't you, darling Fiona?"

No use arguing. "I'm here, aren't I?" Okay, so not very gracious.

"Listen," she leaned in with that smile turning to a tight, feral snarl, dark eyes snapping, "I saved you when Pete Wilkins died and don't you forget it. You owe me, Fiona."

"You kept Petunia's open," I snapped back.

"Same thing." Because, to Olivia Walker, it was.

I grit my teeth and bit the bullet. Of course I did. While Olivia strolled away, smiling and nodding like she hadn't just handed me my self-esteem on a platter.

Turning away again seemed the best revenge. I glanced at the clock behind the bar, hating that I fretted. There was a time I could have cared less about time or anything outside my own little world. But thinking about Petunia's made me think about the two elderly ladies who I'd left in charge back in town. While I was only a fifteen minute drive from the B&B, it felt like a million miles. Now, Mary and Betty Jones had taken excellent care of Petunia's when my grandmother had her stroke, worked there for years before that, handled everything with their stolid determination and quiet grumpiness I knew now came from natural stoic natures and not from actual dissatisfaction. Still, it was one of the busiest nights of the year and they had been left in charge of dinner and the music and…

I really needed to call them. Check in. Not because I wanted a distraction from standing alone at the bar with a decidedly Valentine's Day drink in my hand, a room in the brand-new resort waiting for me upstairs, a free dinner pending and no one to share it with.

Right.

Just when I thought tonight couldn't get any worse, well. It got worse. Right about the same instant Vivian French breezed her way into the bar, her slim, petite figure clad from bare shoulders to toes in pale yellow silk. I had zero doubt those were real diamonds around her skinny neck and in her ears. As for the tiara, honestly, did she look at herself in the mirror before she left her room? Her icy blonde hair wasn't thick enough to carry off a crown, not even artfully piled in precision curls on the top of her head.

Bitter and jealous? Naw.

Personally, I thought Petunia looked better. At least, would shortly. Olivia saved me the agony of the fashion show, at least, opting for a canine version meant to pluck the heartstrings of every animal lover in attendance and hopefully create enough buzz and press to go viral on line. The fact my chubby pug enjoyed her bath, manipedi and general fussing over by the staff running the show more than I did Daisy's attention said a lot about my own priorities.

And hers.

As I stood there glaring—yes, I admit, glaring was involved in my moment of weakness—Vivian's lonely singular state was the only thing that kept me from utterly abandoning my post and downing the entire bar of booze to drown my sorrows. That was, until he walked in. And ruined everything.

I'd spent so much time thinking about asking Crew Turner on a date it sometimes felt like I'd done it already and had been horribly, miserably turned down by the handsome sheriff of Curtis County. Instead, of course, out of utter lack of luck and nervousness about our present relationship's status, I hadn't. If anything, he had to be thinking I was avoiding him, dodging out of shops when he appeared, smiling like a freak and stumbling into things so I didn't have to say hello, hiding out at Petunia's at every opportunity. All because, well, he was hot and I wasn't ready to have dinner with the man who'd once thought I'd killed Pete Wilkins.

Let's be fair here. I wasn't ready to date period. Thanks to all the trust and good will built up by my five-year relationship with my ex, Ryan Richards, ending in cheating (him) and embezzlement (him) and an attempt to pin illegal activity on me (him, strike three), I'd come to the conclusion that men and me? Not the greatest choice right now.

Didn't cut the resentment of seeing him pause next to Vivian looking like a movie star in his perfectly fitted tuxedo. I thought he was attractive in his uniform shirt and jeans. Yowza. Only then did I catch her blue eyes watching me, held still as she smiled and slipped one hand through his arm. And led him away.

So she'd landed him after all. Good for her. I turned to the bar for the last time, downed my drink and accepted another. It was going to be a long, long night.

AUTHOR NOTES

I NEVER MEANT TO be a mystery writer. I started out reading—and then creating my own—science fiction and fantasy novels as a small girl. But it was a Nancy Drew mystery at the tender age of twelve that sparked my need to write for real and woke the creator in me.

Years passed, time spent learning my craft in ways that I hadn't intended—as a journalist, a screenwriter, an improv actor and a hair stylist—telling stories became commonplace and a part of my life even though the dream of being a writer hadn't yet come to pass.

When I found YA through my niece and her love for Harry Potter, I realized I'd been writing the wrong things all along. That the Nancy Drew mystery about a young woman daring to take chances was the kind of heroine I was meant to write about. And, through that understanding, woke Sydlynn Hayle and the rest, as they say, is the **Hayle Coven Universe** (forty-two published books and growing).

But the mystery side of things took a little longer to explore. Though most books have a mystery to them of some kind, designing a whodunit hadn't crossed my mind.

Until a pilot for a TV show I'd been working on popped up in my documents and I remembered how fun it was to write a police procedural based on a fictional city filled with paranormal creatures. **The Nightshade Cases** were born.

But something still didn't feel right. They are dark and full of the kind of nasty things that people do to each other while embracing all things supernatural. Don't get me wrong, I love them. I think, though, from reader reactions, they weren't expecting that kind of cussing, stomping and hard-assed action compared to my YA works.

Fair enough! But I've hated to abandon the mystery writing idea all together.

When Fiona Fleming started talking not so long ago, I listened. Here was the kind of mystery I could not only sink my teeth into, the cozy mystery genre had the kind of lighthearted fun and strong female sleuth I was looking for while staying on the giggle inducing and enjoyable side of the characters I love to write while trying something totally new—no paranormal.

I hope you've enjoyed the first book in Fee's series. There are twelve more to come and, as I explore this genre further, I have a feeling there will be more from other voices.

I'm just having too much fun killing people off not to keep going.

Happy reading!

Patti

ABOUT THE AUTHOR

EVERYTHING YOU NEED TO know about me is in this one statement: I've wanted to be a writer since I was a little girl, and now I'm doing it. How cool is that, being able to follow your dream and make it reality? I've tried everything from university to college, graduating the second with a journalism diploma (I sucked at telling real stories), was in an all-girl improv troupe for five glorious years (if you've never tried it, I highly recommend making things up as you go along as often as possible). I've even been in a Celtic girl band (some of our stuff is on YouTube!) and was an independent film maker. My life has been one creative thing after another—all leading me here, to writing books for a living.

Now with multiple series in happy publication, I live on beautiful and magical Prince Edward Island (I know you've heard of Anne of Green Gables) with my very patient husband and six massive cats.

I love-love-love hearing from you! You can reach me (and I promise I'll message back) at patti@pattilarsen.com. And if you're eager for your next dose of Patti Larsen books (usually about one release a month) come join my mailing list! All the best up and coming, giveaways, contests and, of course, my observations on the world (aren't you just dying to know what I think about everything?) all in one place: http://smarturl.it/PattiLarsenEmail.

Last—but not least!—I hope you enjoyed what you read! Your happiness is my happiness. And I'd love to hear just what you thought. **A review** where you found this book would mean the world to me—**reviews feed writers** more than you will ever know. So, loved it (or not so much), **your honest review** would make my day. **Thank you!**

Made in the USA
Las Vegas, NV
04 April 2021